RUNNING ON FUMES

CHRISTIAN GUAY-POLIQUIN

TRANSLATED BY JACOB HOMEL

Talonbooks

Talonbooks
278 East First Avenue, Vancouver, British Columbia, Canada V5T 1A6
www.talonbooks.com

First printing: 2016

Typeset in Sabon
Printed and bound in Canada on 100% post-consumer recycled paper

Cover and interior design by Jenn Murray

Talonbooks acknowledges the financial support of the Canada Council for the Arts, the Government of Canada through the Canada Book Fund, and the Province of British Columbia through the British Columbia Arts Council and the Book Publishing Tax Credit.

This work was originally published in French as *Le fil des kilomètres* by Le Peuplade, Saguenay, Quebec, in 2013. We acknowledge the financial support of the Government of Canada, through the National Translation Program, for our translation activities.

LIBRARY AND ARCHIVES CANADA CATALOGUING IN PUBLICATION

Guay-Poliquin, Christian
[Fil des kilomètres. English] Running on fumes / Christian Guay-Poliquin ; translated by Jacob Homel. Translation of: Le fil des kilomètres.

Issued in print and electronic formats.
ISBN 978-0-88922-975-4 (PAPERBACK). – ISBN 978-0-88922-976-1 (EPUB).
– ISBN 978-1-77201-054-1 (KINDLE). – ISBN 978-1-77201-055-8 (PDF)

I. Homel, Jacob, 1987–, translator II. Title. III. Title: Fil des kilomètres. English

PS8613.U297F5513 2016   C843'.6   C2015-908253-6
                                                C2015-908254-4

For Jean-Noël Poliquin

this is the story of a man
who wants to see his father again

of a labyrinth running in a straight line
through changing scenery

of abandoned houses
roadside militias
and dreary towns

a story of exhaustion and solitude
of confabulations, encounters, and alcohol

the story of a car crash

I. THE LABYRINTH

A place greater than any single human existence. You might wander through it for years without ever treading the same soil. A place that escapes from the tyranny of touch and sight. Only growing fatigue gives you an indication of the road travelled. A place without landmarks, where the erasure of the outside world is stronger than any memory. Galleries, rooms, intersections; all of them built to confound your bearings. Each hallway is imperceptibly curved and the arc of every single one of these tangled walls follows the curvature of the earth. He who believes he is moving in a straight line is actually drawing great concentric circles. He who turns around cannot retrace his steps.

II. THE BEAST

In the centre of the labyrinth lives a beast.
A beast whose patience strikes fear in the heart
of mortals. A beast who waits for the end with
the determination of those with nothing left to
lose. His silhouette melts into the shadows of
the landscape. His glare is more dazzling than a
mirror. The surprise his appearance causes is the
last spark of life he allows.

III. THE STRANGER

One day, at the doors of the labyrinth, a mercenary come from afar pretends to be made of the stuff of heroes. He is young with a radiant complexion. His eyes are black and his skin the colour of the sun.

He declaims to those who wish to hear that he is preparing himself to enter the labyrinth and he intends to come out alive, his clothes stained with the blood of the beast. Like so many before him, he claims that he is able to outlive evil. To change the true fate of things.

In one hand, he holds a bronze sword, in the other, a spool of red thread.

IV. THE LABYRINTH

The young mercenary steps into the labyrinth. He slowly advances through the narrow corridors closing in on him like blinders. Behind him, in endless meanderings, the thin red thread marks the road travelled so far, and the path home.

Sometimes, the young warrior is startled. He has the impression he can hear someone or something advancing in a nearby hallway. Each time he stops, he holds his breath and scans the hallway around him. Nothing. Only the echo of his leather sandals against the claustrophobic walls.

He knows he is travelling through a place where improbable meetings are bound to happen. But for now, the only movement that accompanies him is his shadow lengthening on the dusty ground.

V. THE LABYRINTH

The day is unravelling, the length of thread slowly unwinding and, with a last shudder, night falls like a curtain, a slowly fraying cord that finally gives way. Hidden by the cavernous obscurity of the labyrinth, the young mercenary sits, counting his every gesture. He is a hunter on the lookout: every time he turns his head he expects to see the beast charging at him from the darkness. But it is a night without glowing eyes, without the sound of hooves and heavy breath. A long night.

PART
ONE

KILOMETRE 0

It was early afternoon when everything stopped. Not a noise to be heard. A sudden darkness in the heart of the engine. My pupils dilated, attempting to pierce the darkness. I laid my tools on the oily ground and rolled out from under the truck.

Voices echoed in the cavern that is the auto shop. Surprise. Jokes. Calling out half-assed solutions. Someone finally shouted to open the workshop door. Others agreed. The heavy pacing of work boots. Then the sound of a toolbox emptying on the floor. The metallic echo bounced against the ceiling, vibrated along the wall before finally landing on the ground.

I hadn't moved yet. Still leaning against the truck I'd been repairing. I dangled my hand in front of my face. I knew it was there, but I couldn't see it. Normally, after a power outage, the generators coughed to life. But now, nothing.

The door was jammed. A few of us made our way towards it slowly, scanning the darkness for landmarks to guide us among the disorder of disembowelled vehicles, pieces of machinery, and toolboxes. Several of us together managed to force the door open. It squealed on its rails as a grey and dreary light washed into the garage. We looked at each other. Our faces, our arms, our clothes were dirty. As always. We stood there for a moment, then went out one by one to see what had happened.

Outside, not a sound except that of the rain. Even the insatiable rumbling of the refinery had stopped. Around us, not a single building seemed to have power. In front of each of them, we made out uniformed blue-clad silhouettes huddled together, scanning the darkened scenery, attempting to stay dry. Snug in the entrance of the garage, our team did much the same. Some tried to figure out if they could see anything outside. Others spoke of examining the fuse boxes. Most of us didn't move. We waited. Two of my colleagues sat down on toolboxes and talked about what to do next. I felt at home under the cornice: I watched potholes fill with water as I smoked a cigarette.

Farther off, foremen were coming and going between buildings. One of them finally came to tell us they were having issues with the backup power system. But the director had said to stay put. Shouldn't last long. Silence was his only answer. He seemed to be waiting for a sign of agreement. Finally, we nodded our heads, so he pulled up the collar on his raincoat and left. A few moments later, three company vehicles rumbled past the garage.

A colleague came near me and pointed towards the refinery's bouquet of smokestacks. Through the drizzle, they looked like immense ionic columns, holding up the clouds. He asked me whether I noticed anything. I stared at him. He told me to look again. That we couldn't see the flames usually shooting out the top of the flare stacks, day and night. I answered that we couldn't see the gas flare because of the rain, that the flames were hidden from sight. He turned towards the others, but nobody cared enough to listen. We were all too busy awaiting our fate, the weight of our steel-toed boots nailing us to the ground.

We suddenly heard the generator rumbling to life. Orange lights winked to life in front of the warehouses. An emergency light turned on inside the garage. But it was still too dim to be able to count the silhouettes of cars left in the garage. I looked down at my hands, tracing the oil stains from my palms to my fingernails. No way we'd get back to work now.

Another group of men was making its way towards the parking lot in front of the garage. Their clothes were drenched, making them seem like shambling scarecrows. We walked out into the rain and asked them if they knew what was going on. But they didn't stop to answer. I shrugged. They'd tell us all to go home now, surely.

We waited a while longer. Then we started up a little committee, asking questions, consulting each other, and soon enough we were talking about other things entirely. What a summer, eh? Everyone nodded. Endless warm days and clear nights, splintered by northern lights. Something never seen before, according to the newscasts anyway. I hadn't seen much of any of it, really. I rarely looked up at the sky. Anyway, from town you couldn't really see them. Because of the refinery's lights.

Half an hour later, while we had begun collecting our things in the half-light, one of the company vans started to make the rounds of the petroleum complex's infrastructure. On its roof, loudspeakers repeated a message. I couldn't make out the whole of it, but its meaning was clear enough. The electrical grid was down. Production would be interrupted for a few hours. Everything would be back on track as soon as possible. Tomorrow, at the latest. For now, we could all go home.

In the parking lot, about a hundred of us climbed into cars, the same small smile on our lips. The smile that schoolchildren wear when they're told news of a snowstorm on the way.

I cut the engine and pulled on the handbrake. The rain had stopped. Getting out of the car, I slowly unfolded, like a pair of rusted pliers. Around me, furrows of mud made their way between the mobile homes. I was glad that my work day had ended early, but I was returning home exhausted, my feet heavy, mired. The screen door slammed behind me. I left tracks on the floor that led to an almost empty refrigerator, from which I grabbed a beer before collapsing into the depths of the sofa. Another day.

On the corner of the table, the alarm clock stood guard over the geological weight of my eyelids. Fourteen thirty-two. I listened to the sounds around me. The refrigerator's muted rumble wandered the room. I stretched my arm towards the light switch. Everything was still working. Good. Too bad. My eyes slowly shut, my mouth opened as if I was about to reveal a secret, then my neck lost focus.

My eyelids slipped open. My beer had remained anchored between my thighs. Taking a long swig I told myself that if I stared at the ceiling long enough a pattern would appear. Sometimes, I could perceive the movements of whoever had applied the plaster, and damp spots were revealed. Cracks became rivers, roads, hundreds of paths like arteries and veins that nourished the drywall. I was also able to distinguish forests, lakes, and the small rectangles of houses. Each time, it was like seeing the same roadmap.

The sky opened and sun streamed into the room, scratching and tumbling onto the yellowing paper of the company calendar, on the brown walls and floors, the soiled white of my arms. I got up and walked to the window, reminding myself once again to turn the calendar's pages. I hadn't touched it in nine months. I should probably replace it. Outside, the whole city like a messy construction site. Everything being built. Everything produced. The population kept growing, but workers left as soon as their contracts were done. Except for a rare few who sometimes decided to stay as if nothing existed outside this oil-producing city. Some days, when the wind blew, you could hear the rumbling of trucks, the clacking of backhoes, and the bellowing of the dinosaur refineries. But on this afternoon, nothing.

KILOMETRE 0

Twenty seventeen. Already. True to form, the alarm clock reminded me I would be working tomorrow. And the day after. Ten hours a day, seven days a week. I took a pot out of the sink, filled it with water, and placed it on the stove. Waiting to toss pasta into the boiling water, I watched for some time the small bubbles growing on the metallic bottom of the pot. Sweat on grey skin.

The sun refused to go down. A yellow washed-out light stretched endlessly over neighbouring rooftops, drying the humid ground. Here, even after rain, everything remained dry and lifeless. Each passing car raised a cloud of rust. A kingdom of dust.

These were the longest days of the year. It was dark four, maybe five hours a night. And the nights were long and sticky. Without sky or dreams.

The pasta was ready. I sat down at the table thinking that I would likely need to catch up on the work left unfinished today. Then I leaned over my plate, poured tomato sauce over the pasta, and ate in silence.

I looked around me, at this place I inhabited like a ghost. One mobile home among so many. Behind the front door, cases of empties formed a pyramid. My clothes were strewn across the floor. Dirty dishes turned molehills into mountains on the kitchen counter. And then there was that hole in the wall, a few months old, perfect copy of my knuckles.

I opened the refrigerator again, but nothing inspired me. The alarm clock claimed it was twenty forty-three. The phone wasn't ringing and I was out of beer. I tossed the rest of my meal into the cat's dish. It would be a change from birds that knocked themselves unconscious on the trailer's windows. I placed my plate on the pile of dishes and made my way to the bathroom.

Water streamed down my body, but I was no cleaner than before. I needed to scrub my arms, my hands, my nails with a brush and abrasive soap to remove oil and grease stains. I got out of the shower and dried myself with a bunched-up towel, still humid from the night before. In the bedroom, I found a pair of jeans and a slightly creased shirt. I dressed in a hurry, took a bit of money out of my stash, counted my cigarettes, avoided the mirror, and left.

KILOMETRE 0

It would be midnight soon enough. Folds of light hung from streetlights even though darkness had not yet fully conquered the day. On the other side of the street, the bar's neon flickered. The music as well, the same as every other night. I smoked a cigarette, apart from the rest. A few others, lurking in the entrance's shadows, spoke loudly and staggered, gesturing wildly. Admittedly, I showed off a little too, leaning against a metal post, a few involuntary dance steps of my own. I dug my hands in my pockets, hoping beyond hope to make some unexpected discovery. But nothing. Not a penny forgotten in the fabric. Only the usual burdens. I turned around and started for home, followed by the sound of my untied boots dragging on the asphalt. Behind me, someone yelled my name, but I didn't turn around. To avoid conversations I didn't feel up to, I always told everyone I was half deaf. By now it was probably true. With years of the racket of pneumatic tools and the steel clang of hammer against metal behind me, of silence only a muted, heavy buzzing remained.

My body knew the path to follow, like a blind dog. Around me, the town slept. Fitfully.

I passed a few workers, dressed in company colours. They began their day when mine ended. Here, there was no time. No, it was more like there were many streams of it. The refinery ran twenty-four hours a day. Each man had his shift. When you went to bed, others were getting up, and like dreams that nobody remembers we crossed paths without seeing each other.

They would be told to go back home. The linear constellation of lights that climbed the tall smokestacks marking the horizon were dark. The grid was still down. At the bar, that was all anybody wanted to talk about. Would we be working tomorrow or not? I heard the emergency teams hadn't solved the problem yet. One of my colleagues said that he had seen on the news that a bunch of similar events were happening across the country. That a number of hydroelectric dams were failing. That reservoir levels were becoming critical and some places hadn't had power for a few days now. Some of the other guys, more worried, said they thought it was caused by a series of terrorist attacks meant to overthrow the government. Supposedly there'd been riots in the streets of large East Coast cities. Incidents in strategic locations. The country's nuclear arsenal on high alert.

On my end, I had no idea what was happening. The streetlights were still on, unblinking, like faraway stars that meant nothing to me. If there had been an attack this afternoon at the refinery, there would have been an explosion, something. A pipeline would have been severed. A reservoir would have burst. I would know.

And, to be honest, I wouldn't care less. Every day was the same. Nothing changed.

At the corner of my street, the toothless craw of one of my company's construction sites. I stopped before it. I examined the concrete framework, steel beams, scaffolding. It looked like a whale run aground, torn asunder by the passage of days and the hunger of nights.

KILOMETRE 0

Back home, I sat down on the front steps, sighing away all the beers I drank. I called the cat, whistling, but he didn't come. He never came. I always left the window to the living room half-open. That way, we didn't need to take care of one another. We crossed paths, sometimes, that was all. And it was enough. I hate cats.

I looked at my car, dormant, a pile of metal chewed by rust and time. Its body was a skin worn thin by dirt roads, salt laid on snowy highways, and the boiling sun of summer. I love old cars. They're easy to repair. When something breaks it can be fixed, one way or another. The engine never dies. A strategic error that car manufacturers no longer make. Supernatural engines. As I played with my keys, the light of streetlamps reflected on the moving pieces of metal. The jangling made me think of the noise of church bells ringing in the distance, far away, from another century.

I missed my first days in this place. We arrived in the middle of winter, completely broke, half in love, half at each other's throats. After months down South, drinking and driving around, we'd managed to find work within two days. She found it in some bar, and me at the refinery. And then months passed without our being able to distinguish one day from the next; making money during the day to pay back our debts, making love at night, amid the glow of cigarettes.

But all of that ended. She left. One night when she couldn't sleep. One night when I couldn't speak. A night like a terrible earthquake. The order of our lives breaking down. And I stayed there until morning, like a bronze statue among the ruins, jaw and fists welded tight, eyes wide, and my heart on the tip of my tongue, watching her pack. She'd put a scarf around her neck to hide her injuries and looked me over, the outline of a bleak, sorry smile on her mouth. It was over. A few moments later her car was turning the corner, raising a cloud of dust. That was nine months ago, more or less. I didn't keep count of the days.

Just as I was about to fall asleep curled up on the front steps, the phone's blare roused me. I walked inside, letting myself be guided by its ringing. In the darkness, I bumped against the corner of the table, tripped and fell right next to the cat. As I got up trying to find the receiver, the cat bounded out the half-open door.

Hello?

It was my father. Yelling on the other end of the line. Again.
I told him to calm down. To speak slower. That I couldn't
understand a thing. That it would pass.

His voice had been the same for a while now. Withered
with age. Sometimes the silences that punctuated his sentences
made me think of black holes, expanding. He hesitated as he
approached each word. Other days, his speech became an unin-
terrupted flood, a great landslide towards panic.

This time he told me that people had come into his house.
That they had wanted the keys to his car, food, money. He
hadn't moved from his rocking chair. They came in and yelled,
loudly, not giving him a chance to answer. There were four of
them. They rifled through his house, overturning everything.
They took the keys to his car, food, and his hunting rifles. They
hadn't found his money though, hidden in the potato bin. Then
they left, joining up with a group waiting outside, before going

into the house across the street. I tried in vain to reassure him. He insisted. They'll be back, them or others like them. I asked him the time, calmly, to bring him back to reality. He stopped talking. Mumbled a little. I don't know, he said, there's no power. He went on to say he should hide and wait. I told him he could wait if he wanted, but he shouldn't hide. And don't forget to sleep and eat. And don't drink. And rest up a little, will you?

This couldn't continue much longer. He needed help. He couldn't live alone in the middle of nowhere, in an abandoned mining town, nearly deserted. My father was sinking with the town, and both he and it were turning into ghosts.

I knew he wasn't doing well. For years now he'd been saying his life seemed to be shrinking, that he felt he was forgetting simple things. That he still drove though his licence had been revoked. That the dark that sometimes filled him had nothing to do with the usual confusion of alcohol and solitude. That trying to find the names of things infuriated him. That he distrusted everyone without knowing why.

And that night, once again, he seemed demented. I tried to reason with him, but he continued, not listening to me at all. A house had burned. People in the streets. His neighbours fleeing their own homes. Then people had come into his house, they wanted the keys to his car, food, money, and he hadn't budged an inch from his rocking chair, they came in, and then they told him … And I hung up.

KILOMETRE 0

To do something, anything.

My father had cancer of the memory. His hands had been resting on the arms of the same rocking chair for far too long. Wearing the same boots and old checkered shirt like a strait-jacket. His cigarettes slipping between his fingers and rolling on the floor. Hunching over while trying to sit straight. Barely able to read and write. I thought this might have been it. He'd crossed the threshold. His memories were tangled. He had hallucinations. Led long, imaginary conversations with my mother. Though he could still yell and scream, I knew that soon I'd have to start guessing words that rested, suspended on his lips. Soon, if it wasn't the case already, he would forget to wash himself and barely eat anymore. He wouldn't know how to hold his fork. His legs wouldn't support him, and he would need to concentrate to put one foot ahead of the other up the staircase. Soon, he would fall asleep still dressed, next to the unlit stove. He would only get up to make sure the blinds were closed. He'd no longer know how to make a decision. His eyes would shine with fancy and vainly search for a place to settle. And he'd no longer recognize me.

I needed to do something. To call him back.

I picked up the phone, called the number, and waited. It rang. It rang for a long time. No answer. I waited anyway. But he wouldn't answer.

As I hung up, the receiver fell from my hand, dangling from the end of its cord. I knew he had no one. Knew nobody wanted him anymore. I needed to do something. It had been years, long years, since I'd been back. So far away. My vertigo a mirror image of the receiver's, gently rocking back and forth, dangling from the end of its cord.

I leaned into the refrigerator again. It was sweating. There was no light inside. No beer, either. Glanced at the alarm clock. It offered no sign of life. Reached out towards the light switch. Nothing. They were probably rebooting the power grid for the whole region. I walked out. Darkness surrounded me. Houses, streets, the entire city plunged into darkness. I could hear voices from the end of the street but saw no one. Then silence.

Everything was black. Everything was calm. Not a light illuminated the small city, except for a cold and blue-tinged glow at the horizon, announcing the day ahead.

KILOMETRE 0

If the power returned and the refinery's flare stack started spitting flames once again, I would need to be at the garage in less than four hours. It would be coffee and work boots. The garage, the humidity of the concrete floor and greasy tools. A truck's innards, a small light bulb overhead. Then, around noon, it would be the hangar with the others, the sandwich, the smell of mustard, the insipid taste of a few old radishes and a can of beer in a Dixie cup. Half an hour later work would begin again, stomach full this time. A cigarette break in the afternoon, the four o'clock blues. At six in the evening, I would head home. A grimy house, warm water in the shower, then a fifteen-minute walk to that bar, full of faces.

If the power was still out tomorrow, then I wouldn't need to work. And perhaps not the next day either. In front of my house, in the fading night, I knew my car was waiting. To leave. Without a word. Without my next paycheque. Nothing held me to this life here. Everything I owned could fit in five or six duffel bags and two large toolboxes. That was it. I also had some money stashed in the potato bin. The road. Kilometres. The heavy hours of early afternoon. The fresh hours of the night. Towards my village. Towards my home. My father. To walk in that door hoping that he might still recognize me despite the years that had etched lines on our faces. To just grab my things without saying a word to anyone and leave without saying good-bye. To drive through the country. To stand before my father, in three days, like a surprise emerging from forgetfulness, defying logic. To tell him everything would be okay, that I was there now. To take care of him.

To forgive a few mistakes, as well. And face my past.

Beyond the dash lights' glow, the road was wide and straight. Like a landing strip ahead, as my car's old headlights faded in the shimmer of dawn. The wind blew insistently against the body of the car, a noise joining the repeated knocking of pistons in the engine, like someone banging on an emergency exit door. Too late to change my mind now. Too late to pretend. To forget. Too late to change the narrative.

I was driving fast. At this hour, no one was on the road. But I couldn't resist snatching glimpses in the rear-view mirror. There was nothing behind me, of course. No orange halo over the town. No flame fed by the refinery's flare stack. No beacon to mark the road behind.

The cat meowed in his cardboard box. I should have left him back there. Especially since he savagely scratched my cheeks when I tried to put him in the box. At least that would teach him to not attack me. And vice versa.

I turned the radio on, looking for a station. Nothing but dead air. No matter. I had a road to drive. I wanted to see my father.

Morning was on the cusp of the horizon. Far away, at the edge of my rear-view mirror, I sensed movement. Slowly taking my foot off the gas pedal and looked back. A thick column of smoke rising up towards the sky still filled with night. It wasn't the refinery. Nor the town. It was farther away than that. A forest fire, probably.

I started off again, shifting gears. The sun finally dragged itself over unimaginatively flat prairies, its first rays striking a landscape where only a few bushes, my car, and strange black smoke seemed untethered from the dusty ground.

Under the noise of the motor and the silence of the radio, I could hear the landscape go by. The barren plains continued, naked in the light of day. Behind, the smoke still wouldn't disappear and clung to my rear-view mirror with its long fingers. I kept thinking of the blaze I had left behind.

I had met my ex-girlfriend three years before in a roadside bar. On the edge of some endless highway that lost itself in the north country. I counted the kilometres. My beer as well. She had come near while I was searching through my wallet. What are you drinking? Let me buy you one. I couldn't refuse.

In that grimy place where women danced naked after midnight, we leaned against the bar as if against a ship's railing. Everything around us was nothing more than faraway horizon. We spoke in flightless sentences, in small hidden looks. Her pink lips. Her soft hands. And her laugh like a waterfall. We were no longer strangers.

That night, in the labyrinth of my car, we eagerly undressed. She was on top, then I was. We were together like on a ship in a stormy sea. And in the parking lot that night, a few honks of a horn somewhere close by, followed by harsh laughter.

I stayed at her place for a little while. A small house next to the highway, hidden by a row of spruce. Three weeks later, the car filled with luggage, we left for the coast, then headed south, careful not to know what lay ahead of us.

The sun was over the road now, highlighting the crack across the windshield. Without looking in the rear-view, I examined the crack until a voice interrupted and asked what I was thinking. Shaking my head, I aimed the car at the white line. Nothing, nothing.

I had left a lot behind, but my past followed me anyway. A beast with a frightful head, horns, a gaping maw.

Travel was a foreign language I knew intimately, but paid no attention to. Instead, I concentrated on the swaying of my car filled with tools. I felt like I was at the helm of a rickety boat on a sea that sought to turn it over.

I followed the same path I had taken so long ago, but in reverse, like you might ascend a long river without tributaries. In the time since, there had been so many detours, so many meaningless encounters, so many dreams weighed down by alcohol, hangovers, money whittled away on the counters of boisterous people, of barmen aching for a few more coins, so many ruses and thefts, so many lies, that I had stopped believing life stories. Be they mine or someone else's.

I drove and I looked at the scars on my hands, on my fore-arms. Marks left by so many work accidents. That screwdriver I stuck in my left hand, barely three weeks ago. The hood that fell on my arm when I first arrived at the refinery. And these cuts I named my daily bleedings, in the shape of a thousand small lines on my knuckles, in the palms of my hand. Every day, a car's sharp metal or gnawing mechanical part shed my blood, mixing it with the engine's dark oil.

I thought of the tools I dragged with me everywhere I went. My toolboxes, heavy, dirty, but oh so useful. My life made of bolts, soldered joints, dust, and grease. Of coffee and cigarettes. Of noise and swearing. Of sighs at the end of the day when I washed my hands clean, slowly, painfully.

Good. Good that it was over.

The last months at the refinery had been especially hard. Under the company's cars and trucks. Again. Just as it had been when I used to work in my father's garage. I who'd promised myself: never again. And the last, fading days with my girlfriend. Who came home later and later. Speaking to me less and less. Who inched away from me, smiling at others. And that mobile home where I'd been sinking, my only company a car, a hole in my heart, a hole in the wall and a bandaged hand, painful, that prevented me from working for several days.

I hadn't been at the wheel of a car for more than a few hours for quite some time. I hadn't been out in a while, really. I felt like I wasn't used to movement anymore. I opened my eyes wide, but my surroundings had become nothing more than a long line of invariable streaks of drab colours. I could distinguish nothing but poorly built fencing that held in a narrow corridor of asphalt.

In the fields on each side of the road, herds of cows grazed. They watched my car with somnolent insolence and the colourless gaze of those who are thinking of something else.

It would soon be noon. The cat was mewling insistently. He desperately pushed at the sides of the box. Three days and three nights of driving awaited me, if I didn't stop too often. It would have been nice to while away a few hours gazing at the scenery. But everything around me was dry and, on this continent, you would have had to drive thousands of kilometres to see anything new. It was easy to believe that I wasn't moving at all, and that nothing existed beyond my windshield.

It reminded me of my father's glassy eyes. His empty gaze, one night at the table, while we ate in silence. I wasn't very old at the time. The only noise was the scratch of utensils on ceramic and the gurgle of a wine bottle being emptied into his glass. It was winter, the days were short in our treeless valley. The town was calm. Boring. People were worried. The mine had closed a little over two months before. Almost everyone had lost their jobs. The few who still kept theirs had fingers crossed, waiting for the other shoe to drop. It was easy to see the scars that up until then we'd learned to hide. Some accused those who'd pushed for the strike of having run the company out of town. Others pointed their fingers at those who, despite a call for solidarity, had replaced the strikers in the mine. But the winners would have no victory. Despite the fact the company had left everything behind. Buildings, machinery, and kilometres of flooded subterranean galleries. That winter, some were still on unemployment insurance, but everyone knew it would only last for a while. Then there'd be nothing. It was the beginning of the end. Those were the only words my father had spoken that night, pushing his plate away after only a few bites.

These days, I recalled my hometown as a place of waiting, of anger, and empty bottles. A village I never wanted to see again. A depopulated place, where house after house was clothed in plywood windows. Houses at whose feet accumulated seasons of dead leaves. Houses with twisted trees in the yard, like those you might see in children's books, when it's time to be afraid. Street corners where kids invented games that could be played alone. Front steps where, each spring, old men and women counted their dead, using the fingers of both hands, and then not having enough. A church and a school with no life left in them, except for shadows of the past. A town where at the grocery store, at the hardware store, at the gas station, only ghosts were named by the few who broke the silence.

A town in which my father was slowly running off the rails, having done nothing for too long. I could understand how a banal and predictable reality could become unbearable with time. And, as I grew older, I began to sense the threshold between lassitude and insanity.

I drove. I drove and my eyes moved to the dashboard. The odometer turned and turned as if it hungered for more. At each pothole, the cat mewled and my tools sang against each other, itching to be out of their boxes. Meanwhile, I shared the dotted line with vehicles I'd never see again.

KILOMETRE 559

The prairies dragged along on either side of the road. On the left, only a railroad filled the empty space, waiting for the next train. Hours frittered away punctuated by tiny villages. I drove through them in slow motion, as if brushing past a ghost.

Just outside one of these villages, I turned my engine off in front of the pumps at a gas station. In the garage door's entrance, a man was seated, eyes towards the sun. Getting out of the car, I walked into his workshop, lost between two horizons. I recognized the disorder. It had nothing to do with the industrial garage where I'd been working for the past few years. It was more like my father's trash heap. A place made of metal, gasoline, and grease where, one day at a time, my father taught me how to put my hands into a car's ribcage.

The man pushed himself up, hands on knees. Fill her up, I said. He made his way to the side of the garage. I heard the sound of an engine starting up and stabilizing. He walked back to me and said there hadn't been any power since the night before. He'd been working his pumps with a generator. Leaning against my car, he noticed my tools on the backseat. He asked whether I worked in a garage. I corrected him by telling him I used to work as a mechanic. He asked me where I was going. I told him due east, east for a while yet. Recradling the nozzle, he said I was lucky, since there weren't many people on the roads today. And supposedly cats are good luck, he continued, pointing at the cardboard box. I paid the man and returned to the quicksand of my seat. When I started my car, he waved in my direction. I nodded, and accelerated. He stayed there a long time, watching me disappear. From a distance, he seemed like a single tree, alone on the plains.

As the car skimmed the kilometres, I began feeling the weight of the afternoon. When I lifted my eyes towards the sky, I saw black birds flying overhead. When I looked around me, there was nothing but wheat fields begging for rain and lifeless oil pumps like iron ravens.

I tried various ways of holding the wheel. My hands moved like needles on a strange dial, finding no comfortable place to rest.

I passed a few cars going the other way, and several trucks. Each meeting lasting no longer than a car crash. But nobody overtook me, and I overtook no one. The pavement lay before me, lasciviously. I drove in the opposite direction of migratory birds. And then, in the distance, a wailing siren. I looked ahead, but there was nothing. Instead, in my rear-view mirror I saw a fire truck and two police cars. I barely had time to move onto the shoulder; they passed me with authoritative urgency. The blast of wind that followed shook my car and I had difficulty staying on the road. Then the red and blue lights began to fade in the distance, getting smaller, before finally succumbing to the horizon. I was alone again, or almost, with only vapours rising over the asphalt.

On the side of the road, truck stops hemmed in by semi-trailers like wrecks around which sleepwalkers prowled. My stomach tightened in a knot. Hunger pulled at my face. I had been driving for a while now, my head full, my stomach empty and, as I kept moving on, waves of fatigue washed over me. But I couldn't flinch, not yet. I was tied to my wheel like a ferryman to his oars. Far behind, I saw the thin line of the foothills forming in the distance. It wouldn't be too hard to believe that I was seeing a mass of clouds, floating away. Or coming nearer.

Before me everything was flat, like the sea.

The road was long and the ashtray filled itself. From time to time, among the endless flat lines all around me, a combine harvester could be seen, sleeping until autumn.

I also saw a number of old barns folded up by time, blackened by sun and abandoned by men. Structures straight out of another time, stitched with rusted nails and drafts of air. With vaulted backs, scrawny shoulders, and skin made of cedar shingles raised up by seasons of winds. Buildings that waited for – with the patience of wood fibre – the great gust that would finally blow them into the brambles and couch grass.

A type of barn that didn't exist in my father's village. A village too far north to be able to grow anything, too focused on what lay in the earth's guts to think of anything but money, and too young, in any case, to have a history of its own. Thirty years of dust, and already bereft of life. Mining towns opening and closing like carnivorous plants.

Along the road, a few signs warned of livestock crossings. The herds grazed the grassy shoulder in the sun, watching me pass. They chewed slowly, oblivious to the numerous slaughterhouses in the area.

When I had reached the age when you think you're no longer a child, my father would often tell me, as if it were his duty, the story of the first time he used a firearm. During the economic crisis early in the previous century, he had lived on a farm. His family raised bison. At the time, they were exotic beasts, and few people had heard of them. In winter, the large snow-covered beasts steamed, whether they were running about or standing still, and scared the children witless. Each morning, my father had to feed the bison, against his will. One day, as breakfast was being served, he still hadn't come back from pasture. Irritated, my grandfather stepped outside, calling after him. He'd barely opened the door when he heard shouts. He ran towards the pen. My father was lying face down in the mud. A bison was standing next to him, foaming at the mouth, though not advancing yet. It was a young bull, no more than two and a half years old. The dominant male was farther away, with the rest of the herd. My grandfather was scared of nothing. He climbed the fence and walked towards his son. The bison huffed through his nose. My grandfather raised his voice, gesturing wildly, trying to scare the animal away. He knew what to do in a crisis, my grandfather, that he did. But this time, the bison charged at him. My grandfather and father were out of commission the whole winter. From bed to couch, from couch to bed. For months, my grandmother worked alone, day and night to care for the injured, her children, and the farm. By spring, my grandfather could still barely walk. My father, more robust and younger, was practically restored. As soon as he felt he had the strength, he took the rifle and several bullets and made his way to the field. It was raining, but he quickly recognized the young bison, apart from the herd. He took his time aiming at its vitals, then shot, repeatedly. The animal fell to the ground, panting, while the rest of the herd stampeded, mad with fear. My father slowly, very slowly, walked towards the animal. The enormous bison had its eyes closed. My father brought the weapon to his shoulder and shot again. The animal didn't react, but a few moments later its eyes opened again, empty and already cold. Each time my father told me the story, he always said he had trudged back home in the pouring rain, walking at first, then starting at a run, until he reached his father's bedside. It's done, it's done, he told him, it's done.

The afternoon wore on, ceaselessly, and the sun pounded down on the body of my car. It was a valiant old pile of iron. Except for a small oil leak. Nothing important. The car moved through the prairie's thin air like an old workhorse pulling its plough.

I saw vehicles passing a car that had broken down on the opposite shoulder. A classic scene: a small, powerful sports car, its hood up, white smoke pouring out. A man waved his cellphone towards the heavens while a woman pulled large suitcases from the trunk. Two young children with worried eyes held each other by the hand on the side of the road. Reaching them, I hesitated a little, but I didn't stop. Didn't even slow down. I had a long way to go; someone else would help them.

Before me, valleys looked like waves. The plains made me think of a landlocked sea whose salt came more from dripping sweat than gushing water. A penned-in space whose froth was not the product of waves but of the thirst gaining ground on the corner of my lips. I could see cars in the distance coming from the other direction, dancing with the horizon, misshapen by heat.

I landed in a small town. Two rows of houses lined the main road. It was the middle of the afternoon. Quite a few people were out, on sidewalks and balconies. Watching the cars go by. Like they had nothing better to do.

I needed to eat. I stopped in front of a grocery store. In the parking lot, a woman dragged two shopping carts behind her, packed like mules. I got out of the car and observed her as she methodically placed the paper bags in her trunk.

I walked into the store. There was no electricity here either, but the bay window let in enough light. The clerk told me they only accepted cash. I nodded and walked along the shelves. They were particularly empty. Cardboard boxes scattered in messy rows. It seemed as though dozens of grasping hands, hurried and clumsy, had passed through.

Skirting by people busy filling their own carts, I found a few sardine cans, a bag of sliced bread, some sort of dried sausage, mustard, and a pack of chocolate bars. There was no peanut butter left, or dairy products, or water bottles. I picked up a few cans of soda instead.

When I reached the cash register, I asked the clerk what was happening. She told me it had been three days since the last delivery truck had been through. I raised my eyebrows and placed my things on the counter. She said that with the power going out in the middle of a heat wave, they'd lost most of their refrigerated products. What's more, increasingly worried customers were beginning to stock up on supplies. As I paid, she told me that two days ago, she had heard on the radio that everything would be back to normal soon, tomorrow, well, soon anyway, and that it was a small problem, a computer glitch or something, and that important infrastructure hadn't been affected. We shouldn't worry.

Outside, I noticed several people standing in front of what looked like a post office. Eyes darkened by the heat, they stared in my direction. As if I had in my possession some sort of clue. They seemed to be keeping an eye on comings and goings. Or getting ready to do something. I quickly hid myself in my car and drove off. Passing in front of them I raised my hand to wave. No one waved back.

As I gobbled up three slices of white bread with bits of dry sausage I realized that my hands no longer smelled of gasoline. That was rare. I'd gotten so used to the smell of gasoline over the years that by now I'd grown fond of it. Despite all the hours spent in the half-light of garages, the smell of gas reminded me of a drink at the end of the work day.

I brushed the crumbs off my jeans and swallowed a chocolate bar. It felt good, I was famished. I was hot. The sun arched over my windshield, like a bird of prey floating on high winds. The salt of sweat stuck to my skin. I felt thirsty as well. I should have realized: soft drinks wouldn't do the trick. I was sick of this nice weather following me, chasing after me. I was thirsty. And the sweet liquid only made me nauseous. Without really admitting it, I hoped the black clouds would catch me, cover the sky and discharge their weight for forty days and forty nights. But for now, in the rear-view mirror, all I could see was a whirlwind of dust following the car, like a laughing madman.

The small town was already far behind. The cat hadn't made a sound in a while now. With the heat, he was probably sleeping. Unless he'd died. I tried to find a radio station but got nothing but static like gnashing teeth. I returned to the silence of the car interior. My foot on the gas pedal, I waited for the hours to pass. I stuck my hand in the gutted bag, looking for cigarettes.

Until very recently, I had confused the dust dancing in sunbeams with thousands of birds, taking flight. But now, at the helm of my car, the dotted line remained fixed on the road, the only thread to guide me.

I continued driving as the clock's hands went about their business, unable to count the hours that passed. I had too many kilometres left to go to begin counting now. Two days and three nights to go. Before arriving home. Seeing my father. I was driving, but still too few numbers accumulated on the odometer. Not enough horsepower roiling through my old pile of iron and rubber. Even if driving for so long sometimes gave me the sensation of flying, I felt like something was catching up with me, following me. And no matter what I hoped to do, I was nailed to my seat, between wheel and gas pedal, at eye-level with the long grass and trash littering the edge of the ditch.

I would have loved to travel at the speed of thought. I'd be sitting next to my father right then, allaying his fears, and mine. We would speak a little. Or stay silent, there'd be no difference. I would look through the window and trust him when he told me how high the trees had grown behind my childhood home.

My house. The house that I grew up in until childhood changed its name. The house that had suddenly become too big after the death of my mother. A few years before my father shouted that I should leave and never come home. Never.

The funeral had been simple. My mother lay there, in front of everyone, her body cold, hands crossed. I remembered it well. The makeup. Eyes closed. Lips sewn. And the murmur of a crowd covering her like a second shroud. I was sixteen. Standing as straight as a cedar post. I couldn't move. Around me, there were too many people. A lot of neighbours. A lot of handshakes. And a lot of whys. Each of them, in low voices, outraged at the thinness of the thread of life. My father was seated, his back straight, a bit farther away. Some were smoking outside, one, two, three cigarettes despite the cold, delaying their return to the flower-filled room. The townspeople came to pay their respects before leaving. Then one of my aunts made her way to the front of the room to speak a few words that her eyes refused to admit. A work colleague whom my mother had struck with her kindness followed. Then my father was invited to speak, but he refused with a gesture of his hand. Soon after, well-dressed men closed the casket and everyone found themselves sitting in the church pews. Outside, a storm had raged for three days.

In the weeks that followed, my father kept repeating that it was impossible, that it couldn't be mechanical failure. That he'd just repaired the car. That he knew my mother's car well. That it had been fine. That it had been in good shape. That it was impossible. That no, no.

In the curve just before the long hill, a few kilometres out of town, the car changed direction and hit a tree at full speed, without slowing. By the time help arrived, my mother had her neck bent over the wheel and was no longer breathing. Traces left by wheels on the asphalt led them to believe that she'd tried to avoid something by pulling on the wheel. Snow had begun to fall. Heavy snowflakes, filled with silence. Not long after, nothing at all was left on the asphalt. The police were never able to identify what she might have been trying to avoid. That was the first snow. It melted only later, much later, when spring returned.

A few days after the funeral, my father returned to work. We told him he should rest. He told us to mind our own business. In the half-light of the garage, lying under the car, hands black from motor oil, he fought against his own darkness. A little later, he started drinking again, that clear liquid that tore at his throat and his voice when he said that life had to go on, after all.

Then the mine closed. Within a few months, several families were gone. Though the number of homes on the market kept increasing, with each new week came a fresh set of false hopes. Rumours of economic renewal regularly burned though town. The company would be bought out. Mining would begin anew. Then elections were held. And months buried weeks and each, in its own way, stayed as far as possible from any sort of promise.

Our home became empty. And cold. There wasn't always someone to put wood in the stove. At supper time, we said nothing, or barely anything, as if we no longer spoke the same language. Only the movement of our forks forced us to open our mouths.

I'd been driving too fast for a while now. And I remembered that there were a lot of cops in this part of the country. And that strangers weren't particularly welcome. Especially those driving around in cars as old as mine. Perhaps I should slow down? But what would be the point? My car kept going. Propelled by mechanical black magic that I knew like the back of my hand.

Despite it all, each time I drew my eyebrows down and forced a bit more gas into the cylinders, I kept my ear on each small explosion, each combustion – as a worried man listens to the sound of his beating heart.

The sun-covered asphalt unravelled beneath my car's used tires. As I reached my first time zone shift, the kilometres per hour became heavier and reminded me that speed was a gale that withered more than it fortified.

My back was bent towards the vehicles coming in the opposite direction. It was easy to believe that it was the first day of summer vacation. Cars, vans, caravans. All packed to the roof. It seemed like I was the only one who no longer wanted to win the west. When I glanced in my rear-view mirror, I could see only the slightly reddened whites of my eyes, burst veins like a thousand criss-crossing roads. My sleepless night followed me and the last time I had truly slept was even further behind. But there were no rest stops on the road. Only a flat horizon, without borders. The shoulder wasn't wide enough. And the ditches seemed deep. I couldn't stop. I didn't want to. I didn't have the time.

I wanted to see my father. To take him in my arms. To hold him tight. Speak with him. Even if after all these years I had the impression of no longer having anything to say to him. We could cover the basics, maybe. Lost love. Work. Alcohol. My story was bland. Ordinary. Diffuse. Faraway already. A mask of anonymity had stretched over my skin for so long that I'd forgotten my own features, except perhaps the dark rings under my eyes, losing their battle to wrinkles. When I finally got there, standing in the doorway, I was sure we'd gaze at one another like two men who no longer recognized the other. Me, tired, used up by road and distance. Him, aged, sour, and quaking. His hair thinning. Bones as fragile as paper. Memory eroded by illness.

The plains I drove across had nothing to offer but ploughed earth, wheat, beef, and a telephone line. The short conversations I'd had with my father over the past few years had all passed through this thin black wire, perched halfway between earth and sky.

Hi, how are you. I'm okay, I'm okay. Everything's fine? Yes, everything's fine. What's new? Not much, and you? A new job. Again? Yes.

In fact, even if, with time, I learned to read augurs, to reveal meaning in coincidences, to converse with my purlieu, this dialogue with the world never managed to diminish the opacity of my solitude. And I was never able to truly name this entanglement of days, geographic hammering, this vaporous path that was mine. Explanations always eluded me. And when it came time to speak, I always preferred to stay silent and listen to the ruined voices that shout in the heads of shipwrecked souls. Conversations with my father were always brief and always the same. We renewed the same promises knowing that they served only to thin the heavy silence we shared so well.

When will you come and visit? We've talked about it already. Ah, right, yes, true, soon. Exactly, soon, maybe soon. You always say that. Yes, and you know why.

Along the road, through the drab mosaic of fields, several grain elevators awaited the harvest. Normally, at this time of the year, tractors should have been everywhere. It was time to bring in the hay and barley. But the fields were deserted. I could see only a cargo train in the distance. It sat unmoving, as if it had suddenly stopped in its tracks, in the middle of nowhere.

Two dozen people busied themselves around the rail cars. They looked like scavengers feeding on a fresh carcass. The sliding doors of some freight cars had been opened. A group was transporting boxes towards a truck parked nearby. Others were stacking bags. All this was happening a few hundred metres from the road where, like so many other cars, I made sure not to stop.

The light of day haloed the asphalt, plunging its deep fingers in the surrounding yellow earth where only shattered hopes flowered. Nothing moved, except for my car, a straight trajectory through unchanging scenery. Far away, under the heavy sky, even the wind turbines dared not turn. Unmoving, as if the heart of the world had stopped beating.

My own heart had stopped beating nine months ago. Or something like it. I'd stayed late at the garage to finish up some repairs. Surprisingly, back then, I enjoyed working a few extra hours. The huge mechanical lair would finally be calm. Without the clinking of tools on the concrete floor. Without useless shouts and raucous laughter.

She walked into the garage. I wasn't expecting her and it had startled me. How had she managed to get in? She told me she knew the guy at the gatehouse.

Everything happened very quickly. I closed the hood of the truck. I washed my hands, my forearms, while she was there, behind me, not saying a word. I was going through my pockets to find my cigarettes. She threw herself on me and, with surprising economy of movement, undid my belt and raised her skirt. We fucked there on the ground, in the dust and the soot, under harsh neon lights. We fucked with urgency, hard and fast. She told me to stay with her, to continue, not to stop, that she wanted to hear me too, that my body was hers, that she wanted to feel the best of what I was, harder. I watched her bend and move, not being able to distinguish pain from pleasure. Her nails. My hands on her breasts. Biting. Our accelerated movements. Her moans. The heat between our thighs. Her staccato movements, as if she no longer had control over anything. Her face contorting. Then a powerful cry, as if she was out of breath. And I fell next to her, sweating, on the cold and dirty concrete, without knowing whether I'd come or not.

I slipped my pants back on, feeling the weight of my cock between my legs. I wanted to smoke. My cigarettes were in the car. Before stepping out, I turned around. She was there. Lost in her thoughts. Her shirt still off. Her skirt around her waist. And she seemed to float in the heights of the hangar, gazing at the softly swinging hook tied to the hoist.

Night had fallen already. The orange halo of the refinery enveloped me. Walking towards the parking lot I told myself, once again, that I liked her. That time spent with her lost its weight. But when I returned to the garage, the room collapsed around me. I couldn't understand what I was seeing. Her feet were beating in the air. Her fists were tight. Her eyes strained towards the ceiling.

My heart was beating in my temples.

I ran towards her, trying to lift her up, but I couldn't unhook her. She kicked me, groaning between muted gasps.

I ran towards the hoist's control pad. I brought the chain down and, following the rhythm of clicking chain links, she slowly collapsed to the ground. I threw myself on her, undoing the chain that was tight around her throat. The marks they'd left seemed like the bites of a wild animal. She coughed a long time, shaking. Then she vomited. I could say nothing so I took her in my arms, thinking of going to the hospital. Once outside, as I hurried to the car, she moaned to me to leave her alone. To slow down. To stop. So I did, for a moment. I held her in my arms. Without ever looking away from the illuminated bouquet of the refinery's smokestacks, she told me it was over. That she didn't want to die but she just wanted nothing to do with anything anymore. This city. This life. And especially me.

I began walking towards the car. I gently lifted her into the back seat and we drove back to my place. The refinery could have exploded then, and it would have taken me days to realize anything had happened.

She left as soon as she recovered. Didn't leave much behind. Except a heavy silence and her goddamn cat.

Trying to concentrate on the road, I realized it had been hundreds of kilometres since I'd checked the oil level. Suddenly, I reeled with the impression that the engine could choke at any moment and that everything might end here, now.

I turned off the engine and got out of the car. My bones cracked as I finally unfolded myself. The air was warm and dry. The sun heavy. The asphalt seemed as soft as roof tar. The metal of the engine crackled. The service station was deserted. Like an island floating in the middle of a drought. I'd been riding so long that when I finally stopped, I suddenly had the sensation that everything kept moving. I understood sailors who suffer from land sickness.

The gas nozzle in one hand, I tried to get the pump to work, but it remained inanimate.

The small shop seemed closed, but the door opened when I pushed against it. It was dark. Anyone there? No answer. I waited. I moved behind the counter in order to activate the pumps. There was no power, though. I looked around me. No cash register, either. I took a few pints of motor oil. Before going out, I shouted out once, to make sure I was alone. Then I took two cartons of cigarettes, three bags of chips, and a jerry can, just in case.

Outside, no sign of life. I pulled up the car's hood and leaned over its entrails like a bored doctor examining a patient. Everything seemed normal. Just not enough oil, that was all. I added some, thinking about all the small drops left behind, like droplets of blood. I told myself a wild animal could follow them like tracks in snow. A part of me hoped some wild thing, an animal or a monster come out of the too-great empty spaces, would attack me suddenly, jump on my back, its mouth watering with a hunger for bloody flesh.

I slammed the hood shut and stretched my legs in the vacant lot of the gas station. My feet were heavy and raised dust that stuck to my sweat like the sea's salty air to the skin of a sailor. I kicked a pebble and heard the metallic clang of my steel-toed boots. There wasn't even a car parked near the building. Only a phone booth drying up in the back. I went in. Lifted the device and put a coin in the slot. No tone. Nothing. As I left the phone booth and looked around me, the place seemed even more vacant under the sun's glare. Around me, everything was so flat that I was convinced I was the tallest landmark between the horizons. I had the impression that something, hidden in a ditch, somewhere, watched me with one eye, like a beast feigning not being ready to pounce.

Walking back towards my car, I came to realize the situation I was in. I was in the middle of nowhere, not a soul nearby, and I had enough gas for two hundred kilometres, at most.

I passed a colony of birds squawking on the turned earth of a field where their only company was an abandoned tractor. As if the driver had run away, upset by a ghost.

Night was approaching. I could feel distance and time melding together, one kilometre, one hour after the other. But couldn't shake the feeling that each minute would never end. If only I could grab them, physically, and dip every minute in a cup of coffee before swallowing it. Black coffee, no sugar. Bitterness in a Styrofoam cup. To keep me awake.

I was driving fast. I love the solitude of motion. Cars I passed were the only presences that populated my journey, but they didn't really matter. Around the road, there was nothing, and that nothing folded itself out before me as I burned through what little gas I had left.

Behind the purring of the motor, the silence was becoming cumbersome. With one hand, I risked opening the cat's box.

I couldn't well leave him in the box until I reached my destination. In the rear-view mirror, I saw him stretch a little before venturing out of his nest. But I remained on guard; they're sneaky little animals.

I would have been happy to listen to the radio. Even if I'd never really cared about what went on in the world around me, I would have liked to listen to the evening news. But I couldn't get a single station. The only thing I heard beyond the rumble of metal was the timed beating of my heart. I'd been driving for a while now, and I wanted to smile at someone. But no matter where I turned, I was all alone, except for my lassitude, my toolboxes, and the goddamn cat cleaning himself.

I recalled the last few years of my life like vague stories told by a stranger in a bus depot restaurant. As if my memories weren't my own. As if the time that I'd spent, here and there, hadn't really existed. Today, all of it bored me. When I yawned, my jaw cracked and my eyes filled with tears.

In the rear-view mirror, nothing remained of the day except for a thin white line between the obscurity of earth and the blackish hue of the sky. It was easy to lose myself in contemplation of this vista that lacked a hill or a silhouette while my car continued on its way. But suddenly, the sound of a honking horn like a tear in the fabric of the air startled me. When I looked at the road again, I was blinded by two large yellow headlights. I pulled on the wheel and avoided a head-on collision by inches. The wheels cried out, strident, stiff, but the car remained unflappable. It knew all about exhaustion at the wheel that flirts with death.

Nothing but accidents to look me in the eye.

If the cat had ignored my weariness entirely, the sudden jolt of the car surprised him, and he jumped between my legs to find refuge beneath the pedals. I gave him a kick. He bristled and tore at me. I tried to keep my eyes on the road while avoiding his wrath. I was forced to stop to confine him to his box.

A laborious operation. As soon as I managed to put him back in his cardboard prison, he began fighting and pushing against the box's weak points, meowing like a maniac.

I tried to calm him down, telling him that it would be all right. Like that voice in the distance, far away in the depths of my mind, narrating my life.

Shut up! Just shut it, will you!

It was hot. The air was heavy. I licked at the saliva that pearled on the side of my mouth and pressed my foot to the accelerator. The cat could complain all he wanted to; as for me, the only thing I wanted was to claim independence before the theatre of passing days turned me into another marionette. I also needed to see my father before forgetfulness held him too tightly in its long, broken fingers. I didn't care about the power outage. Or the rumours. Stories, really. And even if exhaustion had undercut my understanding of things, I knew all I wanted was gasoline.

In a field, a dead tree dressed in black. Migratory birds landed there to spend the night. While I travelled alone. I didn't stop at night, I continued on.

The road lay before me under the wheels of my car and I met only gusts of wind. The cat had fallen silent, exhausted. Finally. I watched the red spiral of the car's cigarette lighter. My hand trembled on the rhythm of the road as I brought the lighter to my cigarette, furiously breathing in. The next moment, when I threw my butt out the window I knew that, behind me, the wake left by my passing was already closing, as if I'd never been there at all.

And once again I let my eyes lose themselves in the rear-view mirror, watching the landscape become softly cloaked by the fabric of night, like a woman putting on a long black dress.

VI. THE MINOTAUR

The star-studded sky dissolves into a flowering blue. Already, daylight pierces the labyrinth like the disembowelled guts of a dying beast. The young mercenary hasn't closed his eyes for the night, and yet he again begins to walk among the countless twists and turns.

Soon, the sun is at its zenith. It crashes into the sand-coated walls of the corridors. The armed young man must squint to keep moving in this shadowless place. He sees bright spots of light each time he closes his eyelids. And when he opens them again, walls are like mirrors. He startles when he thinks he's seen, here and there, a face just like his, wandering among the galleries, lost.

It's hot. Thirst like daggers in his throat. But he refuses to bend. He walks through the bowels of this sleeping volcano, telling himself his sword has yet to find blood. At each intersection, he hopes to glimpse a large open space at the centre of which death, the beast, and he, will have their foretold meeting.

VII. THE MINOTAUR

The centre of the labyrinth seems to grow farther from him as he makes his way towards it. In fact, he wonders whether this beast he's heard so much of is as hungry as the legends say. And if the place he is to be found exists at all. All the young mercenary knows for certain now is that his spool of red thread is running out and, soon, he won't be able to keep going without risk of losing himself.

He purposefully ignores the passage of time. And while he stands there, trying to fathom his instincts, twilight spreads its large hand over the walls. He listens carefully. This is the hour of hungry beasts. But in this place where his promises to regret nothing weigh him down more and more, he hears nothing but his own weariness lurking. And yet, he knows he cannot leave this place without having done what must be done. The night thickens. He tells himself perhaps the beast will show itself only if he pretends to be in the world of dreams. ·

VIII. THE MINOTAUR

Hours pass. The young mercenary feels time breathing down his neck. Huddled in a corner, he can't sleep but pretends to. He wonders if the beast is tracking him. And has been for a long time. A very long time. Like a patient carrion-eater waiting for his prey to topple with exhaustion.

He hears a noise. Behind him, not far away. Someone, something is coming closer. The beast. He knows it. He can feel it. Close by. A few sword slashes away, crouched in the night.

The young mercenary slowly grips his weapon. And in one movement jumps up and throws himself in pursuit of the monster through the interminable galleries of the labyrinth. He howls like a madman and the beast flees on its hind legs. He distinctly hears the sound of its hooves hammering the labyrinth's earth, pulling away ahead of him. In the thick obscurity of night, the young mercenary calls on the gods to give him the strength and courage to track his enemy and slay it.

He moves ahead like a hunter, ready for a fight, ready to throw himself at the throat of anything that might stand in his way. Each dark corner is a potential threat. Each intersection, a danger.

Suddenly he feels a warm breath on the nape of his neck. He turns, slashing his sword. But his blade cuts only air, knocks on the ground and vibrates through his bones. Shaking himself he runs off down the corridors, certain that he's about to finish the vile beast once and for all.

Night ends and, deep in the galleries, one can still hear the echo of his laboured breathing and the metal of his sword repeatedly striking walls of stone.

PART TWO

KILOMETRE 2053

I needed to fill my tank. The needle was about to fall off the dial and I was beginning to imagine the worst. On the side of the road, I saw a cardboard sign. GAS. With an arrow. I followed the sign to an old warehouse, a bit off the road. In a parking lot, a dozen cars had gathered around a parked tanker. I waited. Without my headlights, you couldn't have a seen a thing. A man came towards my car. He turned on a flashlight. Good evening. Good evening. We're only taking cash. Okay. You'll need to wait half an hour, there are people ahead of you and it's a slow process. Fine. He half-waved in my general direction and headed back to the tanker truck. I put my head out of the window. How much is it, exactly? There hasn't been power in a week, so it's five dollars a litre. I nodded non-committally and turned off the engine.

The scene was a strange one. Headlights. Shadows around the truck. The purring of motors. An empty lot. And, in the distance, the landscape sometimes lit up by cars travelling in the night.

I was waved over. Fill her up? Yes, and the jerry can as well. I took the bag carefully nestled under my seat. Around me, faces drawn, and furtive, cautious looks. When they told me the tank was full, I paid and left. Back on the road, I counted my reserves a few times over. Even if I now knew that my savings would melt away faster than expected, I was still relieved.

But the gas tank's needle had begun to fall again. On the side of the road, streetlights like meaningless, functionless totems. The farther eastward I went, the clearer the effects of the power outage became. Like a curtain pulled over the land. A puddle of oil spreading over the ground. Or maybe as if everything had been orchestrated, following a precise plan I'd been unaware of. Anyway, it was summer, at least. A few days without power wasn't the end of the world.

Little by little, stars winked out and the pink fingers of dawn scratched at the horizon, announcing another clear day. A hard blue day. Without any wild animals in the shapes of clouds. Without a place to let a fertile imagination roam.

I remembered the slap I'd gotten when I told my father that my mother visited every night to sit at the foot of my bed and speak with me. He told me to shut up and not go around inventing stories. I'd been serious though. And he had been too.

Each additional kilometre per hour increased the vibration of my car, but the land moved too slowly for my taste, as if held in place by gravity. I wanted to see my father, no matter the cost. To see him before his memory collapsed completely. While it might still be possible to hear him before the curtain of insanity irrevocably fell. And, especially, to see him after the distance of years that had held us from each other. On the fingers of one hand, I counted the thousands of kilometres that I still had to drive, and on the other, the sleepless nights to suffer through. Meanwhile, sleep had become a waking dream between two rotations of the odometer. A small town driven through, unnoticed.

The cat started mewling again. But this time without energy. He must have been thirsty, hungry. I'd take care of him next time I stopped.

Pastureland extended into the morning's half-light, and my headlights diluted the sky. The landscape flat and unchanging. As if I'd simply circled back to my starting point overnight. Despite the growing familiarity of the featureless landscape, I convinced myself that everything disappeared behind me as I drove forward. As the bags under my eyes deepened.

I remembered my father as he was that spring when the insomnia of grief printed itself on his face. One day, I went to the garage. It was around dinnertime. I saw him from a distance, standing in front of his auto shop. He hadn't yet seen me when he made his way towards the carcass of the car that had been towed to the garage after my mother's accident. I knew he spent long hours staring at the twisted metal, his fists in balls. I walked in his direction, his back still to me. He clambered into the car through the space where a window had been. He started the engine which, strangely, still worked. Then he pressed the accelerator, his hands tight on the wheel. The engine ran hard, pistons clanging loudly. I stayed completely still, my face contorted and hands sweaty, listening to the thundering noise. I imagined the needles and gauges whirling senselessly. The whole scene seemed interminable. I feared everything might explode. Then the engine's sound changed. Like teeth grinding together before breaking. A strident, dry sound was heard. And everything stopped. Not a noise left, now, except for the whispering of white smoke flowing out from under the hood of the car. My father didn't move. I advanced a few steps and called out to him, timidly. At the sound of my voice, he clumsily extracted himself from the vehicle and came to me. He asked how my day had been. Fine, I said. And we walked back home as if nothing had happened. That night, he swallowed his meal in two bites. When he lay down on the couch, I heard him murmur something. There, it's done, it's done. Then he slept for two days.

Before me, the road became confused with undergrowth. Not a soul in sight. I zigged and zagged over the dotted line. From time to time, my small steel mule shook its head and brayed, all the while stubbornly persisting through the wasteland of kilometres. Deep in my seat, I kept slowing down without realizing it. I had to press down on the pedal to keep myself awake. I was eating kilometres like a wild cat, a few bites at a time, tearing apart its prey.

Suddenly, in the distance, in the shy twilight, at the moment where everything becomes uncertain: a silhouette. At an intersection in the middle of nowhere, a shadow with its arm out, thumb raised high. At the deepest moment of the night when you believe the sun will never manage to pull itself over the horizon, at the coldest hour, at the moment when I felt the most alone trying to push through the distance before me: someone else.

I neared the silhouette. The sun was on the point of rising, but it was still dark and I couldn't distinguish it well. I noticed only a large travel bag at its feet. A shame I had no room. Or time to stop. It was better if I travelled alone, anyway. A passenger would just slow me down.

As I neared, she slowly lowered her arm, as if guessing I was a lost cause. A gust of wind.

I braked and stopped the car on the side of the road. The cat started moving around in his box and managed to free himself. In the rear-view mirror, I saw her approach my car. I tried to catch the cat but he was too agile for me. She ran to my window, coughed once or twice, and knocked. A woman, thirty years old, more or less. Black eyes, black hair, long black shirt. With a large green duffel bag.

I signalled to her she should wait, giving me time to grab the cat, but she didn't understand my disorganized gestures and opened the door. Before I could say anything, the cat jumped between her legs and disappeared in the roadside grass.

I looked at the woman. She was pretty. Pale under reddened cheeks. Very pale. She bent forward at the waist and, in a breathless voice, asked where I was going. Without answering, I told her to catch the cat. I got out of the car. We searched the tall grass, looked in the ditches. I scanned the fields around me. I whistled after him. Then we waited.

He wasn't coming back. I knew that. But I couldn't just leave him here, like this.

My cat.

I shook my head and told the woman I was going east, very far east. She answered that she had a long way to go to get to the city, and that a long way east was fine with her.

While I tried to find some room for her on the passenger seat, she glanced at the chaos that reigned in my car. Sorry, it's a total mess and it smells like cat. She climbed in next to me and placed her bag between her legs. She fussed over her hair for a moment and thanked me.

I told myself that the imaginary beast that followed me would probably stop for a moment here, lift its snout to smell the air, prick its ears as it frothed at the mouth, raise a cry, eat my cat to satiate its appetite, and continue its quest with increased fervour.

We started up again. Each time, it was the same thing. The clutch was capricious and I needed to push the engine hard before changing speeds. My hands trembled on the wheel. I didn't know whether it was the irregularities of the cracked asphalt, the hesitant direction of the car, or because my entire body was quivering.

The woman next to me caught her breath, letting out a few sighs. From the corner of my eye, I could see her chest rising, falling. You're okay? She said yes yes, I'm okay. And both of us fell into the abyss of the road opening before us, with the uncertain whistling of the air on the car's chassis slowly increasing, a rising tide of silence.

The sun was slow to rise. You've been waiting for a while? The woman said yes, not really, well maybe a little but not that much. Then she blew on her hands to warm them.

You're cold? She gestured no, adding that the morning's humidity took her by surprise, was all. What are you going to do in the city? Without looking at me, she said she was going home. But that it was a long story and she'd appreciate if I didn't ask her about it. Not right now, anyway.

The dried-out fields were laid out before dawn like a great sacrifice. The sun, finally ready to emerge, dragged with itself a sky dipped in blue. Birds left their temporary perches and once again formed asymmetric sails ready to defy the plains. At my side, the woman watched the prairie flow alongside the car.

I was no longer alone.

We drove. When the sun finally showed itself fully, its light assaulted me. For all my squinting, the sun forced me to avert my eyes. The woman went through her bag and took out a pair of sunglasses. She handed them to me saying they would help. Good idea, thanks. And, in fact, I put them on and the sun backed away, a single step. I smiled and charged towards it. I glanced at the rear-view mirror. I had black eyes. Black and anonymous. The marks of weariness were gone. Even if the morning's sun leaned into my forehead with all its strength, and even if the afternoon sun would be worse, I felt better.

The woman eyed my pack of cigarettes that slept between the windshield and the dashboard. Help yourself. I lost my lighter, but the lighter socket worked. Behind my sunglasses, my eyes darted back and forth. I tried to remain anchored to the dotted line while watching her light a cigarette. Following the curls of smoke slowly rising from her mouth before slipping through the half-open window. She was beautiful. Her face was tight with tiredness or something I couldn't quite identify, but she was beautiful. She had small, delicate hands, resting on her thighs. Her legs seemed strong, toned and rounded. The skin of her neck disappeared under the large collar of her shirt. And the curves of her breasts could be guessed despite the dark cloth.

Already, the sun was high in the sky and the horizon shivered with heat as if it was about to break. But I was no longer alone. And even if we said very little, it would erode the mountain of time still left to drive, just a bit faster.

The road ahead shone in the light of the day, and the dotted line now climbed into us, as if we were smoking the same cigarette. I had the impression that if I closed my eyes, the car would stay on course. All around us, nothing but fields besieged by pitiless drought. For two months now, it hadn't rained on the country's vast prairie. Beneath the yellowing grass, we felt the ground pulsing in waves of heat.

The woman turned towards me. She mentioned the scratches on my cheek. I told her it was nothing. She answered that she'd never liked cats either. Then she asked me what I was doing here, at the helm of the car. Surprised, I lifted my foot from the accelerator a bit. Our bodies were propelled slightly forward. Her voice resounded in my head. I'd been alone for so long that a physical presence next to me seemed impossible. Her eyes. The lines of her face were fine and dark. Her skin was pale and delicate. Her eyes. Her immobile lips were pink and defined.

Her slightly hollow cheeks betrayed her last few nights spent under the cold blanket of anxiety. Her eyes.

I told her I was going to see my father. That I hadn't seen him in some time. That he was ill. His memory in pieces. He'd known what had been coming for a few years now, but had said nothing. I guessed he'd made lists. Hundreds of lists. A man like my father couldn't conceive that he'd forget everything, one piece at a time. That he would have to die twice.

Just over the horizon, we could see the next town's water tower. I've always loved the tall steel structures. So large and yet so frail, seen from afar. As if always about to topple over.

The woman was still looking at me. She kept the conversation going, and asked whether my trip had something to do with the power outage. No, well I don't think so, I said. But like everyone else, I couldn't ignore it. Everywhere, people were on their guard. Gas was expensive, and at night, not a single light to show the way.

She told me that her life had been so filled with the slow death of routine that she progressively developed a taste for catastrophe. Sometimes she'd dream about witnessing some serious accident. Other times, she would imagine herself able to cause chaos by intent, by simply looking at things. She'd stare at planes as they flew overhead, hoping they'd explode; gaze at the foundations of bridges, hoping they'd crack. She always saw storms in dark clouds. She hoped she would be in a great city when all the lights finally turned off so she might hear the shrieks and cries in the distance while, in the sky, the stars would finally regain their rightful place. She paused a moment before adding that all of it was a ridiculous fancy, really, and nothing ever happened.

She said that in the small town where she'd been living, the power didn't just fail all of a sudden. There'd been cuts here and there for a while. Especially at night. People had started getting used to it. The blackouts would last a few hours and then the power would come back on. Until, one morning, it just didn't. And food started rotting in refrigerators. Telephone lines stopped working. Prices increased rapidly. People locked themselves up in their homes, worried and suspicious. But that wasn't why she left.

She told me that she couldn't deal with the desert of her apartment anymore, of the familiar disorder of her kitchen and the quicksand of her bedroom. That she couldn't wait anymore for a man who came in late at night and put his gun on the bedside table. That the daily life of a trafficker, the drunken nights playing the hero, and the dirty sheets stained with nicotine and sweat were too much. She was tired of doing nothing more than rolling empty bottles on the floor. She didn't want anything to do with this life. So she left like a wild thing in the night. Three days ago. Early in the morning. Without saying goodbye. Before he returned home, even. She took with her jewellery that she grabbed out of a drawer and the money that had been left on the bedside table. And she was thankful for this power outage that gave her a chance to disappear without a trace. Hidden in the baggage compartment of a bus.

She told her story without once moving her hands. Only her lips moved. And the blacks of her eyes trembled. She finished by saying it'd be best if she never saw him again, him or any of his friends. They were crazy enough to try anything. I stayed silent for minutes after that. Until I saw police lights flashing on the road ahead.

Shit.

Three police cars blocked the road ahead. There didn't seem to be an accident. I took my foot off the accelerator and told the woman that my papers were somewhere in the glove compartment.

I lowered my window and stopped my car at the roadblock. Five officers were milling about. There was no one and nothing else in the area. The closest town was some ten kilometres away.

An officer came over, scratching his head. The others remained leaning against their vehicles, continuing their conversation. The officer bent over to look through the window, scanned the bazaar of my car's interior and took off his sunglasses. I kept mine on.

Where are you going? East. To do what? Visit my father. You've heard about what's going on? Yes, a little. Given the situation, we're asking everyone to turn around.

I looked at him and didn't add anything. The officer sighed. He seemed more tired than I was. My seat belt wasn't buckled, but he didn't seem to care.

And your trip is important? Yes, my father is sick, I've got to see him.

A truck rumbled up from the other direction. The officer turned his head towards it while one of his colleagues made his way up to the door on the driver's side. I looked straight ahead, seeing the single police car I'd need to get around to resume my journey. The truck slowed down, the driver stuck his head out of the cab and yelled something, and the policemen signalled him to continue. The officer turned back towards me.

Okay well, be careful, avoid cities and hope your car doesn't break down. I'm a mechanic. Good for you, just go, go on if you must. Okay, just a question, though, what's going on exactly?

We're not sure. We're having problems with our radios. We haven't had power for more than a week. The police force here is overwhelmed. And we've heard that they've had trouble keeping crowds under control in the cities. Total confusion. Some people are taking advantage of the situation and looting. Others take the law into their own hands. We've received the order to filter outbound traffic and block new entries to the territory.

The policeman stopped talking then, his eyes downcast, he seemed to carefully weigh his words.

The latest news from the city is worrying. The army has taken over. We haven't had contact with our superiors for forty-eight hours now. The only advice I can give you is to turn around. If you keep on, all I can say is be careful.

The officer straightened up and knocked on the hood of my car. I started the engine, drove around the police car, and accelerated to cruising speed.

We drove quickly through a lifeless town. A few sleepy houses and three shops beside a crossroads and a rail line. The woman said she was looking forward to seeing what was happening in the city. I watched her from the corner of my eye, without adding anything. The silence of the road engulfed us. Like a sealed letter.

We were driving at full speed on the deserted road while the afternoon spread over the car roof. A few hills began to appear beyond the carpet of the prairies and the colour of the land-scape was slowly changing from yellow to green. The asphalt flowed ahead in long curves. Stunted conifers, here and there, punctuated the horizon.

Despite what the officer said, everything seemed normal. Houses on the side of the road. High-tension lines. Cows grazing in fields next to barns. Whether it was some revolutionary coup, a nuclear accident, or a technical problem, the ditches, telephone poles, signs, and bales of hay seemed deeply indifferent.

The day progressed and we sank gradually into the fabric of the seats. As if the journey didn't need us. Grasping the wheel, I felt my vision blurring under the weight of exhaustion, but I didn't let it show.

The woman attempted in vain to find an FM channel that still broadcast. She was raging against the machine, insisting she wanted to listen to music. Any music. Just to give us a bit of pep. I remembered a car I once drove that broke down in similar circumstances. We'd been driving for a while, music blaring. The cooling system gave out and we didn't notice. Then the cylinders failed because of the heat. We only understood what had happened when the car simply stopped, all of a sudden.

A roadside sign indicated a hundred kilometres to the next town. The woman asked me whether we could stop soon. That we'd been driving for a long time now. That she needed to go. That it wouldn't be long.

Suddenly, she gasped and pointed towards the sky. I leaned over the steering wheel and saw thousands of birds darting and racing in the sky. White on one side, black on the other, they zigged and zagged as if not knowing which wind to trust. They twisted and turned and continually changed directions. In perfect concordance and utter disorder. The woman said it was a beautiful sight, mentioned how close they flew to each other. She loved the movement of birds. She said that usually it was towards the end of autumn, just before the great migrations, that you saw these sorts of gatherings.

We were bowed under the windshield to watch the air show passing over and over again before us, skimming the fields. Then, a black line, a muted sound, and a slick of blood decorated with feathers. I turned the wipers on. The whole windshield awash in red. The woman receded deep into the cushions of her seat. My heart tightened, and despite my squinting I couldn't see a thing. I stepped on the brakes. The worn disks squealed and did what they could until the car stopped on the shoulder's gravel.

We stepped out, not looking at each other. Not a vehicle in sight. The sun was heavy. The air stagnant. On the windshield, the blood was already coagulating and browning. With an old work shirt I wiped away what I could. And while the flight of birds moved on under the hard sky, the woman stepped into the fallow field, told me not to look, and crouched to piss.

The plains stretched into hillsides scattered with sage and dry bushes. In the distance, we began to notice conifers. The sun was beginning to go down and shadows were slowly spreading over the parched ground.

We'd been driving for more than an hour and hadn't yet reached another town. The windshield was still streaked with blood, but it looked like traces of mud. Through sunglasses, the light seemed more golden than it was. The only intersections we passed were dirt roads that lost themselves in surrounding woods, looking for water.

A light wind seemed to blow across the landscape as if over too-hot soup, and the high grass on the sides of the ditch joined hands thanking the sun for sparing them for the night.

Checking the gas level, I noticed that the engine temperature was abnormally high. I slowed down and listened closely. It was too hot outside and I didn't feel like walking. Especially in this part of the world. The needle was still climbing. I turned towards the woman. We have to stop, we have a problem.

I slipped the car into neutral, turned the engine off, and let the car glide to a stop. I opened the hood and leaned over the engine. It was crackling slightly, but it didn't seem to be over-heating. I examined it carefully. The oil level was right. More or less. The belts were in the right place, still tight. The radiator's fan wasn't stuck. There was still enough liquid in the cooling block. But the problem had to be there, somewhere. I got on my knees and looked under the vehicle. Nothing. Except for the usual droplets of oil.

The woman joined me. We needed to wait until the engine cooled before I could do anything. She ran a hand through her hair and told me that we needed to move on from here before it got dark. I knew that.

While I dug through one my toolboxes, a truck went by in the other direction. Without slowing down. I shrugged. If it wasn't the radiator's thermostat, it could be the water pump. In the first case I'd simply need to take the thermostat out and plug the wires back in. The radiator would then be able to cool the engine as usual. In the second case, I would need replacement parts. For that, I'd need to drive to the next garage, stopping every fifteen minutes to make sure the engine didn't seize up and leave the car a useless carcass.

I couldn't take any undue risks. And I couldn't delay. I slipped under my vehicle with a pair of pliers and electrical tape, took out the radiator's thermostat, plugged the wires back in, making sure I didn't burn myself on the still-boiling metal, stood back up, and said that it was okay, we could go on.

We got back in the car. I turned the key, blasted the heater on, and slowly accelerated, keeping an eye on the dashboard indicators. A few moments later, the woman asked whether we'd make it. Yes. But we would have to be patient if we didn't want to walk the rest of the way.

The town was forty kilometres up the road. It took us two hours to make it without leaving the car behind. And a bit of luck. We reached a gas station standing guard at the outskirts of the town. I turned off the engine, glad it hadn't overheated. And that night hadn't yet fallen.

We stepped out of the vehicle. A few cars were moored in the parking lot, next to a tow truck. Four people smoked cigarettes in front of the door to the gas station that doubled as a convenience store and post office. A bit farther off, in the garage's shadow, two men seemed to be working on a Jeep engine. I walked towards them.

One of them quickly turned around and made his way towards me. I asked him if I could get some gas here, and whether he might have a water pump. Keeping his eyes hidden under the visor of his cap, he signalled that I should come nearer. Under the persistent gaze of one of his companions, he asked me a few questions. I answered.

I've come from out west. I'm tired and I have a lot of road ahead of me. No, there was no power when I left. Yes, the road is serviceable. Except for a police roadblock a few hours from here. No, my radio doesn't work. No, I've got no weapons on me. Yes, I have money, enough for a tank of gas and a water pump.

The man lifted his cap and signalled I should follow him. I accepted, knowing that the woman would stay in the car.

When he turned around, I noticed what was likely the shape of a revolver under his shirt, tucked into his belt. Pulling away, he told me that he wouldn't make his offer twice. I followed him into the darkness of the garage, vaguely nodding towards the scrawny kid working on the Jeep. The place looked like a battlefield. Shelves were pushed to the ground and emptied. Parts and tools were strewn all over the floor. The man told me they'd found the place in this state. He took out a flashlight and illuminated the spilled mess on the floor. You know anything about engines? I told him that if I found the parts I needed, I could figure something out.

Kneeling on the ground, I searched around for a water pump and a radiator hose. The man stood behind me. He shone his light, saying nothing. Moving a box of drive belts, I noticed a few shells on the floor, among the bolts. Despite that, the smell of humid concrete, oil, and metallic dust reminded me that I was in my element.

A few minutes later I came out of the garage with a water pump model that would probably work with my old car. The man escorted me to my vehicle and watched me drain the cooling system and quickly get the tools I'd need together. I removed the traction belts and hoses connected to the radiator. With an economy of movement that came from experience, I immersed my hands in the engine, unbolted the water pump, and took it out. The man came closer. He was taking off and replacing his cap. I examined the piece I'd just taken out of the engine. The small turbine that moves the antifreeze had come out of its axis. I tried to turn it with the edge of a screwdriver, without success.

It was a rare type of mechanical failure, but it happened. I held it out to my observer, who took it without knowing what it was. I bent over the engine again to install the new water pump, but it wasn't the right model and I had to jury-rig a few hoses to install it correctly.

When I finally straightened up to put water in the cooling system, I realized that now six of them were watching, saying nothing. I gathered my tools and started the car to make sure my repair held. Looking at the engine turning, I wondered for a moment where my co-pilot was.

It looked fine. I closed the hood and turned off the engine.

I made my way towards the group and asked whether they had gas. They told me that nothing was working anymore. That you had to pump the gas directly from the cistern. Like we used to do with water, a long, long time ago, the guy said. While I wiped my hands on the work shirt that I'd thrown in the back of my car, the man with the cap noticed the dried blood on the cloth. You had trouble too? No, nothing serious. The man nodded a few times, then told me I owed him a hundred dollars for the parts and two hundred for the gas. I looked through my wallet, my face going blank. Two hundred, that's all I've got. You're a mechanic? Yes. Good, we need someone like you here. I can't, I've got to keep driving. It's three hundred or you're not leaving here.

I looked at him for a moment, then changed my mind and got the money from my stash under the seat. He counted up the bills then gestured to one of his companions. The young man disappeared behind the garage and came back with two full jerry cans, which he emptied into my gas tank. I was offered a cigarette and a lighter that I discreetly dropped in one of my pockets. We smoked without saying a word, watching the dull, immobile landscape. Deserted houses. Our dirty faces. The last few rays of sun of the day. A van broke the silence, dragging a dust cloud behind it. The man with the cap took advantage of the movement to ask me a new round of questions.

So there's no power at all, even out west? Right. It's been a while? I don't know, three days, maybe. Here, it's been fifteen days, at least. Uh huh. It's pretty serious, more than half the people I know have left. Because of the outage? Yes and no, when the radio signals went out and phone lines stopped working, some people got scared. Right. Then there was the problem with the garage owner: he didn't want to sell gas. To anyone.

I said nothing. When I threw my butt on the ground, the man stepped on it and advanced towards me.

I hear it's chaos in the cities. Especially out east, where they haven't had power for even longer than here. People are afraid. Things are getting more tense. You have to be careful. And even if a lot of people are running, we prefer getting ourselves organized here and not spending too much time on the roads. We've got everything we need here, except for a real mechanic ...

I thanked them politely and offered the hint of a smile. Turning around, I was happy to see that the woman was already in her seat. She gestured for me to get in. My bones popped and readjusted themselves to the dusty, smelly habitat and, a few minutes later, the garage was nothing more than a flickering stain in the rear-view mirror.

I thought about what had just happened. Nothing important in the end, considering that car was repaired and we had gas to drive through the night, as well as a new lighter.

We shared dry bread and a few sardines. The woman prepared bite-sized pieces for me that I swallowed almost whole. The road began drawing curves among sharp green hills, almost yellow. Like the colour of my eyes, hanging on to the road. Like those of my father, hanging on to the names of things.

I asked my companion whether she believed what people were saying. About the power outage, about what was happening out east. She answered that often people like to imagine the worst. To see it in everything. As if imagination could decide the course of things.

In fact, I was most worried about my father. Even if we had a lot to say to each other, I knew he could be difficult sometimes. And that he saw me as a stranger. Sometimes I had the impression that his illness was some confabulation, that it was simply convenient. And that I was the one heading straight for a wall.

I didn't think I'd actually spoken, but I realized too late that I'd thought out loud. The woman spoke softly in my direction, telling me that everything would be okay, that I would know what to do when the time came. With some effort, I managed to smile. I felt the weight of the food I'd eaten in my stomach, beginning to ferment. I hoped it would pass.

I looked at my hand, clasping the wheel. It seemed light years away from my body. I could use a beer. I turned towards the woman. In the heart of my weariness a thousand words came to mind but I couldn't find a single one to say. She was so beautiful. I finally told her I didn't have much money left. She assured me that she'd help out. I didn't need to worry about it. Then, she put her head out the car window and let the evening wind dance in her hair. I mostly looked at the small eddies that timidly lifted her loose shirt.

The sky was pink, orange, red.

After leaning back in she looked at me, hiding behind the tangles that had appeared in her hair. I concentrated on the road as if I'd never stopped looking at it and slowly pulled the car back between the lines.

She suddenly confided that she couldn't take being anonymous anymore. That she just wanted a bit of recognition. That she was tired of being a nobody. That she was like a bird that knew how to imitate the calls of wild beasts, but it wasn't enough. That she no longer wanted to hide the scars on her heart. That it was because of this, really, that she'd left and found herself next to me.

It was dark now. Night had fallen. Before us, only the weak light of the headlights pushed against darkness. The woman said that her former partner had always sought to live his life without ever needing to kneel before a master. Together they tried things that had exhilarated her at the time, but meant nothing to her now. I thought about the mask of sobriety I had put on and told myself that, on my end, the only glory I knew was the slightly dull one of waking up each morning.

The woman stretched out, and between two yawns told me that I'd been driving for a long time now and that I must be exhausted. I told her that she could trust me. That I knew what I was doing. That I was made of sterner stuff.

She didn't push the issue. Her deep, slow breathing cradled me until thirst came back to haunt me. I drove at irregular speeds. Each time my eyes wandered to the dashboard, I pressed the accelerator once again to catch up with lost time. I wanted to drink something fresh. Something strong. Something to help keep me awake. When I listened carefully, I could almost hear the sound of a beer being opened. I no longer watched the clock. I thought of other things.

Shadows weakened under my headlights and we moved through the abstract landscape of night, following the reflectors that lined the road. Occasional passing cars reminded me we weren't alone. It reassured me. The woman slept. I wanted to lay my hand, softly, on her thigh. But I feared she would open her eyes. Curse me out. I remained still, grasping at the wheel like a thief at his prison bars. In any case, with my callused hands, I would have never been able to sense the softness of her skin.

My arms were weak. I could barely keep the car in the right lane when we passed a semi-trailer. It felt like my car was too light. That it could, each time it crossed paths with a truck like that, be pulled into its slipstream.

The woman fidgeted in her sleep, then opened her eyes. We were deep in the night, but she told me she hadn't slept. She bent over, found her bag, and took out a few notes.

She said we should stop in the next town. That we should find a motel room for the night. That she would pay, that she had money. That I needed to sleep.

I knew she'd end up slowing me down.

I told her that I didn't have the time. That it was risky. That I preferred to go on. That I wanted to see my father. That I could still drive. Sleep could wait. Dreams as well.

She answered it was crazy. Crazy and dangerous. I told her I was a big boy. She said I looked like a ghost. I looked at myself in the rear-view mirror. But I only saw the pallor of my face and the shadow of my three-day beard.

She offered to take the wheel.

I repeated that everything was okay.

She refused to listen.

I insisted.

She said, You're lying.

So what?

KILOMETRE 3112

I was pinned under the weight of my blankets while my eyes wandered across the desert of the ceiling. I studied the immense surface as if I needed to cross it.

The woman slept next to me. We had found a room in an abandoned motel. Almost abandoned. Not a light, not a sound, but a few cars in the parking lot, including one parked sideways, its hood up. I parked mine in the back, so it couldn't be seen from the road. There was no one at the front desk and the room keys were hung on the wall in front of us. Without asking any questions, we just walked into the small, simple room. A door, a window, a bathroom, a bed. A bed where I felt the heat of the woman slowly flow over me despite the imaginary border that separated us.

Night followed its course. The sheets slowly imbibed my sweat. The room filled with my breath. When I closed my eyes, I saw myself at the wheel of my car. Sleep had given up on me.

I sat back up and lit a cigarette. I could imagine the woman's body under the white sheet. I could guess her curves. Her thighs. Her ass. Her breasts. But her face was hidden by the black of her hair.

Head against the wall, I took a deep drag of my cigarette as if I was inhaling myself from the inside. I watched the cigarette tremble at the tip of my fingers. Exhaustion was a scar in the depths of my eyes, but I gazed at that small red ember burning in the night. In the darkness of the room, I could almost believe it was an emergency exit.

I swept my eyes across the walls, scanning the enclosed space as if something hid here, around me, somewhere. An animal, a stranger, a monster. Something. I almost looked under the bed to quell my fear.

Suddenly, on the other side of the wall, I heard breathy cries and a squealing mattress. We weren't alone. The door was locked, the drapes pulled. And nobody knew we were here. I didn't need to worry about people fucking as if nothing in the world existed. As if life was beautiful. I closed my eyes and tried to think about something else. When I opened my eyelids and took a long drag of my cigarette, I heard my insomnia whisper that it was my cigarette that was smoking me.

A draft. It came in and out of the room, moving the drapes. Without making any noise, I pulled myself out of the bed, put my shirt on, and looked outside. Except for a few muted laughs from the next room over, everything was calm. I left the room and tiptoed along the side of the building until I reached the restaurant adjoining the reception. It was dark. I bumped into the side of a table, stopped a moment, listened. Nothing. I lit my lighter and walked towards the counter on which a few stools were placed, legs pointing at the ceiling. Behind the counter, I found the beer refrigerator. All in all, I found a dozen bottles that I deposited in a box. Before leaving, I looked the place over, drinking a beer. Everything was strangely clean. As if the small restaurant would open tomorrow. A few candles on the counter and the absence of a cash register betrayed that impression. I left the restaurant and returned to the motel room with care, not wanting to clink the bottles together and attract attention.

Everything was silent in the darkness of the room. The woman hadn't moved. I lit a candle from the restaurant, opened another beer, and closed the bathroom door behind me. In the mirror reflecting the flickering flame, my red eyes burned like embers in the middle of my ashen face. My veins popped on my forehead, on my neck. I leaned over the sink, two inches away from my own face. Ten years. Ten years of brushing my teeth every morning and seeing, in one mirror or another, my face hardening with the passage of time, my face like a fortress, with squinting eyes and lines left like cracks in weather-beaten stone. I lifted my chin and observed the small scars that neither the shadow of night nor my three-day growth could mask. My beard in which a few white hairs revealed my age. How many times, returning home at dawn, had I closed a bathroom door behind me to shave? Despite my clumsy gestures and the cuts, my face exposed by the razor blade always made feel younger, less drunk.

Even if there was no hot water, I would have liked to take a shower, but I was afraid someone might hear the water running. I turned around to take another beer and was startled. The woman was there, standing in the door opening. She came near. So close to me. I could feel her breath. I held my own. She placed a finger on my lips and told me to let her. Then, without protest, I let myself be undressed like a snake lets the sun shed its old skin.

Her cold hands moved across my body and pulled me to the floor. Her lips were soft. Her tongue as well. Our bodies ached for each other as if they'd already met. Her nipples hardened under my touch. My head fell back when she bit on my ear. And as soon as I took her shirt off, her long hair stuck to her skin like the stripes on a wild animal.

The sheets cast the movement of our staggered breathing and my body moulded her shape. I was the negative of her silhouette. A thirsting shadow. I'd left my exhaustion in the car, the woman's touch had burned it out of me.

She turned and faced me.

She asked why I wasn't sleeping, what I was thinking of. I said nothing and let my hands softly survey her body. The white of her skin melting into the white of the sheets. My blood pumped through my veins, a physical presence. Desire pushed me against her again. But she told me to calm down, to hold her tight and to try to sleep.

Sleep.

I tossed and turned a bit, then reached for my cigarettes.

I awoke in the labyrinth of sheets. The woman was no longer there. I quickly got up. The insistent fingers of day scratched at the sides of windows. It must be late. I got up, pulled the drapes, and was blinded by daylight throwing itself at me, claws out.

I put on my clothes. Slipping my belt on I caught the side of the ashtray that fell on the floor and shattered. With my foot, I pushed the cigarette butts and pieces of glass under the bed and the dream I'd been dreaming came back to me, in a rush.

Through the bay window, I watched clouds dangerously heaping up over the refinery. Among the smokestacks and reservoirs, there were skyscrapers, highways, parks. Then a long vortex of wind came down from the sky, churning within itself. Like in the movies. It advanced towards me, destroying everything in its path. Cars, company dump trucks, pedestrians. Far away, the asphalt danced beneath the squall. Then the rain came down. Close by, trees writhed and kowtowed to avoid breaking.

I turned around and, in the room where I stood, a crowd of people demanded answers. We heard explosions. The bay window shattered. Wind rushed into the room, pushing against the walls. Doors slammed open and shut. I recognized no one. The tornado was there. I knew that everything depended on me. But when the time came to act, I saw my father, shivering, in a ball on the floor in the middle of the increasingly frantic group of people. I wanted to cry out his name, but each time I opened my mouth I called after someone else. I walked towards him, trying to catch his eye. After that, I wasn't sure. It became hazy.

The woman opened the door as I was about to leave. Face to face with her, I smiled sheepishly. She held two bags, filled to the brim. She greeted me and said there was still plenty of good stuff in the restaurant kitchen, that there were two or three people outside, but they'd probably not seen her.

We sat on the bed before a meal of a few less-than-fresh vegetables, sliced bread, apples, peaches, canned hearts of palm, and a chocolate bar. We ate in silence, taking care to save some food for later.

Suddenly we heard three sharp knocks on the door next to ours. We listened closely, our eyes fixed on the breadcrumbs on the sheets. Through the wall we could hear a man's voice. He was calling out to open the door. Another voice called out it was time to pay. We looked at each other. Then, with as little noise as possible, we quickly gathered our things. I walked towards the door. Someone spoke next door. He said he didn't understand, that he'd already paid. Impossible, a voice replied, and anyway he still had to pay again.

I took the woman by the hand, gesturing that she not make a sound. I opened the door and pulled her along with me. In the parking lot a group of four people carried boxes to a van. Nearby, two men interrogated the occupant of the neighbouring room about a hockey bag and guitar case. I moved faster, but we had barely come out of the room when one of them called out to us.

Where do you think you're going?

I lowered my head and turned towards him. He demanded that we pay for the night. I told him I had no money on me but we could go to the bank. The man walked towards me, asking whether I was making fun of him.

What's in the bag? Food. Show me. Come see for yourself.

While the man looked me over, I saw, over his shoulder, our neighbour who, still facing his improvised creditor, discreetly winked at the woman. As soon as I leaned down to open the bag, he pointed his finger at the people working around the van and asked what they were doing. The man I'd been speaking to turned around and, surprised at not having noticed before, made his way to them, taking a handgun out from the pocket of his coat. At the same moment, our neighbour knocked the other man down with an astonishing punch, took his bags, and threw himself in our direction, dragging us with him.

Running, I told him my car was behind the motel. He asked me what direction I was going. I gasped, towards the coast. The east coast. He said that was fine with him. We jumped in the car and I started it immediately. The tires shot gravel behind us and we sped through the motel's parking lot. There were several people around the van. And boxes spilled on the ground. We heard shouts. Then a gunshot. But I kept my foot on the gas.

I slipped into fifth gear. The motor beat its drum at full speed. My eyes glanced at the dials, everything was in order, we were back on the road. I turned towards the woman. Breathing hard, she told me that she was all right. The man who followed us was seated in the back, cramped between my tools, my bags of clothes, his hockey bag, and his guitar case. He laughed, saying that we sure had gotten the bastards, then thanked us. He admitted that it was a nice coincidence. That his car had died in front of the motel. And he hadn't been sure what to do next. That it was kind of us to pick him up since he wasn't a mechanic and would've never managed to repair his own car. He leaned forward, his face between our two seats. The woman sighed and closed her eyes. The man was of indeterminate age, greying temples with sharp blue eyes, clear whites, not at all bloodshot. He added that, in any case, he would be with us only for a few hundred kilometres. That he'd be our conversationalist. That our journey with him would be a quick one. But could we, perhaps, tie some of the luggage on the roof to make a bit of room for him?

I hesitated, scanned the mess in the backseat, and said we could stop, but only for a moment. Once the car was on the shoulder, I took a rope out and asked him to give me his things. He refused and threw two of my bags out of the car, telling me that should be enough. I watched him for a moment. He was playing with me. Then he tipped his head towards mine and whispered that I didn't want to know what was in the guitar case.

While I tied the rope as solidly as possible, he got out of the car and gave me a slap on the shoulder. He told me everything would be fine. That he knew the area. I told him to get the jerry can from the trunk and empty it into the gas tank. That we would need it.

The small red car was fully packed and speeding along under the black eye of the sun. My bags were tied to the roof like a hunter's kill, the body of some animal paraded on Main Street at the end of autumn. My arms stretched out, I held the wheel without effort. As if it wasn't me driving. Once again before the parading kilometres, I looked at the dials, knowing I'd fallen behind. I also knew that even if I could drive as the crow flies, I still had a lot of road ahead of me.

The asphalt shone and the scenery slowly changed. Forest now dominated the landscape. The horizon tightened around us. We passed a few small rivers and lakes. Beside me, the woman said nothing. Through the window, she watched transmission towers all in a row, like pilgrims frozen by lightning.

The man sat in the back seat, among my tools and trash. One hand on his bag, his eyes on his guitar case, he said it was hard to think of life before all of this. That the power outage had changed everyone's lives. That those who didn't show fear these days were the most dangerous. He'd heard about riots in the cities, mass movements that had nothing to do with popular revolt. It seemed that thousands of people were crossing bridges on foot to become refugees in the surrounding countryside and the smoke of fires could be seen from kilometres away. He added that he'd been told all sorts of stories. Whether power plants had been the target of attacks or not, one thing was certain, this was the worst power outage since electricity was invented. Fifteen days now – maybe more out east – with nothing at all working except for the combustion engine.

In the mirror, small glance after small glance, I tried to evaluate the man behind me, my eyebrows raised. While his clear gaze was radiant, his halting demeanour betrayed something strange. He asked me whether we could turn on the radio. That he wouldn't mind listening to a few oldies. That music was a rare treat these days, even when you were a musician. While the woman searched for something other than dead air, I answered that the radio didn't work, that at least I hadn't been able to find a station since I'd left. The man smiled. Watching the woman continue her fruitless search, he said he was happy to have met us. That he knew the area and could tell us the places where we could rest and resupply without fear or worry. I thought about the motel and the beers I'd left behind. I almost wanted to turn around.

The man said that it wasn't the first time he had travelled cross-country. Nor would it be the last. Like a sailor, he was used to the swaying of the road, the dead-end hours of the night, and the flickering horizon.

He said that these days you crossed the continent like you used to cross the ocean. With a bit of luck, and a lot of patience and stubbornness. He would have loved to have been alive during the great explorations. Sailing over the horizon before losing yourself in a forest. It would have been worth it, even if his dream meant a short life and an anonymous grave.

He told us that, one day, a long time ago, a man had embarked on a galleon hoping to explore the great open spaces he'd heard so much about in the ports of his own country. But after two hard weeks of sailing, the wind stopped blowing. Heat oppressed the crew, made worse by the incessant swaying of the open sea under the ship crippled by a windless ocean. Creative and courageous, the young man threw himself in the water to freshen up. He swam for a little while, enthralled by the infinite sea around him. When he turned his head he realized that the current had pushed him far from the ship. The swells were high, making his return doubly strenuous and lengthy. The crew was waving at him from the bridge. They threw out a lifeline, though so close to the ship that it didn't really shorten the distance he had to cross. The young man was valiantly fighting the abyss when shark fins suddenly appeared in the waters near the ship. He thought himself lost. With each movement, he anticipated having a leg or an arm ripped from him. Then as if by magic, a light breeze quickened the current and brought him considerably closer to the ship. The other sailors shot their muskets around the exhausted swimmer, scaring the sharks. Then, as soon as he had his hands on rigging, they dragged him up onto the bridge, where he fell to his back, half dead. The captain walked over to him and told him he'd be left to be eaten by sharks next time. He didn't like his ammunition being wasted.

In the rear-view mirror, far away, I saw clouds thicken from white to grey to black. In front of me, though, sunlight pierced the silhouettes of trees and danced on the asphalt. From one glance to another, the black mass behind us seemed to gain ground while the man continued his story.

Around the same time, not long after the discovery of the New World, a captain managed to convince some hundred men to join him for an expedition. They left the old continent a few months later, heads full of promises. But the crossing was long and difficult. As soon as the crew landed, many were ready to return home. Reminding them of the commitment they had made, the captain gave the order to burn all the ships except one. That night, flames ate through the wood of the ships, under the horrified eyes of the sailors. The next day, while high tide was dragging bits of burned wood on the beach, the captain spoke. He told the cowards to leave right away on the last ship with a story as their only reward. Then he spoke to the rest of his men, telling them they no longer had a choice. Glory had a price. They had to follow him now and obey. The next day, at dawn, they would take their weapons and armour and march into the jungle. They'd only return when they had enough gold to buy the crown off their king's head.

The trees were closing in on us, and we charged headfirst into the landscape like animals fleeing without knowing why. The road was deserted. We still had a good amount of gas, we could keep going for a long time.

Taking a few cans of beer out of his bag, the man said that the day was far-gone enough and that it was probably noon somewhere. I nodded in approval. The woman pretended to not have heard. The man handed me a beer and let another fall at my co-pilot's feet, telling her that it was better to drink than be thirsty. As I swallowed my first mouthful, he took the opportunity to compliment her on her beauty and apologized for talking so much, saying he was only trying to distract her. When I looked in the rear-view mirror, I saw him raise his beer to the health of survivors.

Enormous stumps, branches left willy-nilly, and conifers lying on their side – all abandoned to the slow decomposition of battlefields – decorated the forest around us. From time to time, in a hollow between hills, the roots of trees swam in stagnant water. Trunks rose from these swamps, without branches or with barely any, like tall silhouettes with indistinct limbs. Long scrawny shadows watched the thin incision of the road in the belly of the immense boreal forest.

Drinking his beer, the man said that we all end up coming home, one day. That all three of us were returning whence we came. Despite nothing being certain anymore. And that our hopeful folly was that time hadn't eroded anything in our absence. As if erosion was some otherworldly phenomena, for others but never for us. Then he raised his voice to say that all of it was ridiculous. Life went on, with or without us. People died and disappeared. We never really found what we were looking for. Memory was only good for spinning a great yarn.

Like another ambitious captain, he continued, who so long ago had wanted to avoid a dangerous crossing by looking for a shortcut through northern waters. The captain had also hoped to find a new maritime passage. And with it, glory. After a few weeks navigating along the coast, he met an ice floe. He faced one of two possibilities: turn around or circumvent the ice by sailing out to sea. Turning around at this point in the expedition was inconceivable to him. And so he inventoried his supplies again and pushed his ship onward between the icebergs. But after only a few days, the sailors could well see a crag of ice closing in on them. The ship was immobilized, and soon enough they understood that they'd be prisoners of this frozen sea until spring. And winter was terrible. Wind. Cold. Hunger. The endless white that confused sky and earth. And constant bickering that wasted precious energy. When spring finally arrived, they were all looking south and had been for some time. Weak, demoralized, gums red with disease, they prepared the ship. When the ice bank finally broke open and the ship could sail again, they abandoned their dead and, famished, began their way back. But poor weather followed them. Every time they advanced any distance at all, the sea would push them back by just as much. One night when the sea was calm, the captain was taken by a strange inebriation that had nothing to do with wine. He threw himself into the deep blue of this sea of ice and salt, leaving behind his crew to fight the wind. Few of them ever saw land again.

The man said he couldn't care less about promises of return. That he'd never believed in anyone's return. Even more so these days. However, he said, it doesn't matter where you go, or how hard you tried to erase your memory, remembrance always gripped you where your skin was most tender. Then he lit a cigarette that he puffed on as if he could breathe at last.

On my right, the woman took care to stay as far away as she could, leaning against the window. When she turned her head towards me, her eyes held the dryness of the prairies we'd just left. Are you okay? She said something softly, but I couldn't hear her over the tireless voice of the man behind us.

You always had to doubt true stories and official narratives. The more the truth of a story was insisted upon, the more corrupt it was. A few years after the war, in a southern sea, a destroyer had run aground on some high shoals. It had been quickly taken by a storm and, after a four-day search, the authorities concluded that the ship and crew were lost. But two weeks later, on a beach, the waves spat out a survivor. Burned by the sun, tortured by hunger and thirst, he was transported to a military hospital. Soon enough, the press made him into a national hero. Twelve days on a makeshift raft, in the middle of the sea, without water and a book as his only food. Even though no one was allowed to visit him, his story was on the tip of everybody's tongue. The miracle man who ate words. Then months passed, and time and forgetfulness played their usual role. One day, however, the story returned to the surface. The ship had sunk, surely, but no reef existed where it had torn open. Several journalists tried to find the survivor, but the army had disposed of him somewhere. Meanwhile, a story of survival at sea was published by a daring publisher. A fiction. It told the story of a sailor who survived his ship's sabotage as it smuggled weapons destined for a neighbouring country crushed under the heel of some hellish dictatorship. Almost two weeks floating on a makeshift raft. Surviving beyond all hope, drinking rainwater, and eating the pages of a book. The captain's diary.

I felt like I was in a four-wheeled aquarium. I listened to the man tell his story and thought about my own tale, which wasn't much more than a series of accounts noted on a calendar. A banal story. Common. Narrow. Heard a thousand times through the din of bars and train stations. Or in the masked confusion of books. The story of a man travelling through an empty, borderless place, knowing that the lies he faces are often far more real than truth.

We passed a few gas stations with handwritten signs indicating they were bone-dry. Weathered, the ink on a number of them had washed out and we guessed the words far more than we could read them. We needed gas, and fast.

Behind us, clouds still gathered and darkened on the horizon. Here, however, the sun was heavy and a strong stink of bitumen rose from the asphalt. It felt like the asphalt became sticky as we passed over it, liquid, viscous. As if the car slowly sank into the tar of the road, or that our journey was slowly swallowing us up, with the patience of a reptile swallowing its prey.

For more than two hours not a single car passed and we met a line of vehicles all packed to the roof, coming the other way. In the cab of the pickup truck that led the way, five men watched us approach. We passed by them, feeling ourselves under surveillance. A convoy of a dozen cars, three vans, and a school bus. They too had luggage tied to their roofs but, unlike us, they seemed to prefer not to travel alone. They were like a caravan, preparing to cross the desert.

I emptied my can of beer and slid it under the seat. The man told me from the backseat that people were fleeing westward. Life wasn't easy in the cities. They were running from what awaited us on arrival in the city. A few days prior, someone told him that the soldiers tasked with protecting electrical infrastructure were requisitioning all the food they could find and establishing fenced-in camps. Emptying every cargo truck and train they could get their hands on.

The man gave me another beer, telling me he'd always dreamed of robbing a train. That he'd often clandestinely ridden trains. And that he'd learned to hide from security guards who patrol marshalling yards. And yet, at the time, he'd always been fleeing something. After all, victors always find a place to call their own.

The strange convoy disappeared in the dark sky of the rearview mirror. Without a moment's breath, the man continued, saying that, in the end, you always get caught. And that if you didn't want to finish your days dead in some ditch on the side of a highway, you had to learn how to get by and sneak in anywhere. Through doors and windows left unlocked at night, along the walls of huge mansions, among thick crowds ... In speechless beds, under countless gestures, in the drum of washing machines, along deserted roads, in obscure one-ways where the hours are long in the darkness of the baggage compartment of a bus.

I remained silent. Meanwhile the woman seemed to be lost in the passing of anonymous scenery, all woven of needles. I had the impression she was listening distractedly to our new passenger. And that she let herself nonchalantly lose herself in the details. I turned towards her several times and caught momentary glimpses of understanding that revealed the space between her body and mine to be like continental drift, constantly shifting and unpredictable. My father always told me you couldn't trust people who talked too much. My father.

The more I looked at him, the older the man in the backseat seemed to become. His grimaces seemed to be well-practised mimics. He exaggerated. When I asked him his age, twice, he was careful not to interrupt his story. I stopped talking and soon enough his voice became one with the engine's vibration, and I could no longer distinguish anything but the woman's breathing and the long, slow whistling of the road. I missed my cat. Even if I hadn't liked him. At least he didn't talk.

KILOMETRE 3677

We arrived at the outskirts of a small city. I slowed at the sight of a barricade made of two huge tree trunks and several metal barrels. A dozen men were on guard. They were armed. I turned towards the man in the backseat. What do we do? He told me to advance slowly, hide my beer, and just talk as if everything was normal. He said I shouldn't turn off the engine. We would need to move quickly if it was a trap. I sighed and stopped the vehicle a few metres from the militiamen. As one man approached the car, examining the bags tied on top, the man in the backseat told me to not mention him at all. I lowered my window.

What are you doing around here? I'm going east, I need to pass through. What's waiting for you there? My father, he's sick, he needs me. Do you have a way of communicating with him? No. Where are you coming from? Out west. And there's no power over there? No, not that I know of. Did you have trouble making your way here? Some, I had to find gas, food, and a place to sleep. Do you have weapons? No.

At my side, the woman was like a statue. Her eyes were empty as if she wasn't really there anymore. In the backseat, the man listened, without saying anything. For once.

What are you carrying? Clothes, tools, a bit of food. Do you know anyone in town? No. You have no weapons, is what you told me? Right. Sure, yes. Can you open your trunk?

The militiaman had a look and came back to my window.

Fine, you can drive on in, but you can't stay more than a day if you don't have any family inside, that's the rule. I just want to get on my way, there's still a lot of road ahead me. Fine, here's your pass, don't lose it.

As the other men opened up a path for me through the barricade, I called out to the militiaman. The man looked me over, suspicious. I told him to come back, for a moment. His colleagues observed us, arms crossed over weapons strapped to their shoulders. I asked him what was going on. He looked at me before leaning against my door.

Listen, he said, you know as well as I do, probably. We haven't had power here for three weeks now. At first, like everyone else, we thought it would come back. They were saying all sorts of things on the radio. That it was caused by bad weather up north. A minor mechanical failure. Then they started talking about a major incident at a hydroelectric dam. Human error. Maybe some conspiracy. The government gave new explanations every day. Then, all communications just failed. Since then we've gotten a bit of news, here and there, from people passing through. Like you. A lot of people speak about a wave of attacks. Of incredible violence near big cities. And completely disorganized emergency assistance. But it's nothing more than rumours, we can't be sure of anything.

Another car arrived behind us. It stopped while two militiamen walked towards it. In my rear-view mirror I could clearly see bullet holes in the windshield.

You know, the man continued, I heard that there was fighting between the army and people who didn't want to leave their homes. And supposedly our neighbours are putting up refugee camps on the other side of the border. You hear so many things you just can't know what's true anymore. Here we're organized, trying to get ahead of whatever trouble might be headed our way. We're already thinking about what we're going to do over winter. The city is secure. We control every entrance and exit. And we've imposed a curfew.

Behind me, I saw the militiamen helping the driver out of his vehicle. He was injured. They laid him out on the ground and called for the first-aid kit. The man talking to me straightened up. Surveying the scene developing behind us, he told me to keep moving. That I could stock up on gas and food in town, at reasonable prices. One last thing, he said, I don't know what you've seen or done on the road, but things are good here, so don't go around town professing doom and destruction.

Understood? Understood.

KILOMETRE 3679

We entered the city by way of a large boulevard lined with car dealerships and superstores. Parking lots were empty, traffic lights didn't work, but there were people in the streets. And on their faces we could see emotions other than panic and fear.

It was a beautiful afternoon. We slowly drove down the main street, looking at the arrows on cardboard posters nailed to telephone poles. GAS. CLOTHES. FOOD. TOOLS. NEW ARRIVALS. There were few cars on the road. Most people were on foot or bicycles. We wanted to pass through unnoticed, but the road dust caked on my car and the luggage strapped to the roof betrayed us as outsiders.

I turned off the engine in front of a gas station. Tacked to a post, a sign informed us that every ration ticket was worth three litres of gas. On the other side of the street, three small tents sheltered fruit and vegetable stalls. The woman told me she would take care of the food and slammed the door behind

123

her. I turned towards the man in the backseat and told him he'd reached his destination. He looked me over, watched the woman walking away and told me he still had a ways to go, and that I was his driver. A young pump operator approached, asking me for my ration ticket. The man whispered to me not to move from here, that he would find us a drink for what little road was left.

I don't have one. You just got here, right? Yes, as you can tell. If you don't have a ration ticket, you've got to pay by the litre. Okay, no problem. It's twelve dollars a litre. Really? Yes. Right, okay, I've got enough, the pumps are working? Yes, the generator is out back. Fill her up, then. I can't, we got a ten-litre limit.

I stared at the young man.

I've got a lot of road behind me and a lot more left to go. I need gas. I've got money. Do I need to say anything more?

He smiled, telling me there was no reason to raise my voice. That he understood, but I should keep it quiet. We shook hands.

Carefully filling the jerry can, the young man asked me questions about the outage. As if I knew more than him. I told him that three days ago there'd been power out west. Surprised, he asked me how that was possible. I shrugged. Then, lowering his voice, he insisted. He asked what I'd seen on the road.

Fields and roads, and a few abandoned cars. That's it? Yeah, pretty much, except for a few details. What details? Nothing important, people are a bit worried, but it's going to be all right. Right, it's going to be all right, it's summer.

I paid him with the cash on me and searched the car to count up what money I had left. My two companions were still wandering, somewhere. I decided to quickly examine what the man was lugging with him. In his hockey bag, I found a sleeping bag, clothes, a few books, toiletries. Nothing surprising. However, the contents of his guitar case were another story entirely. Methodically organized were hunting clothes, vacuum packed food, a small coal water filter, a first-aid kit, medications, a deck of cards, a revolver, two boxes of bullets. I closed everything carefully. Raising my head, I saw the young man at the pump observing me from the corner of his eye.

The woman came back. We placed the water bottles and food in the back. She told me we could hold out for more than a week with the supplies she picked up. But we would have to be careful, since it cost her a lot. I nodded.

The man still hadn't returned. I started the car and told the woman that nothing held us here any longer. She warned me that that might not be a good idea. That I didn't know what he was capable of. She said I should be patient, that everything would be fine. I grasped the wheel and let my head loll back. At the same moment, the man opened the back door and sat down, a case of beer on his lap.

Not long after, we arrived at the roadblock at the far end of the city. Quick questions, short answers, waves, and good lucks. As soon as I shifted into fifth gear, and the trees began flying past us, the man offered us a beer. We accepted. And the sky darkened.

The light was fading. The green of trees becoming black. Fog banks were landing among the swamps around us. Before me, the road rolled out its red carpet along curves and vales. Fatigue buzzed constantly in the back of my head. I could feel the alcohol in my veins keeping it at a distance. We were now crossing through the endless forests of the north. Except for the militiamen as we left the city, we'd seen no one, only trees and lakes.

The man hadn't said anything more than a few words since we'd gotten back on the road. He kept looking outside, drinking his beer. I asked him to play us something on his guitar. Silence is fine, I told him, but it lacks a bit of flavour. The woman smiled. The man answered that he was missing strings on his guitar.

That's a shame.

But he said that he always had another story to tell. Spring hadn't yet begun, it was still the end of winter. Two shapes on a snowmobile, father and son. They were crossing a lake when suddenly the ice gave way. Though stricken by the countless daggers of frozen water, the man had enough strength and quick enough reflexes to throw his son out of the fissure. Before foundering in the dark waters, he told him to turn around and get on his hands and knees so the ice wouldn't collapse under him a second time. That the town wasn't very far. That he would always ... Night fell as quickly as the man disappeared. In shock, the young boy was unable to leave. He was found only a few steps from the broken ice, the next morning. Unfortunate survivor. His voice gone, cold to the bone, but alive. It happened not far from here.

The woman asked the man whether all his stories were true. After a mouthful of beer, he told her that truth was only what you decided to hold on to, to believe. That if you didn't know how to lie you were still a child. And that children didn't live very long. Then he stretched towards me and asked whether we could stop a moment, one minute, not very long at all.

Standing on the side of the ditch, the man said that, in the old days, when it was time to place the markers that separated two pieces of adjacent land, fathers would bring their sons with them. They then buried a large stone at the agreed-upon border and, in the very next moment, each father gave his own son a beating. So that they never forgot the place.

I coughed a few times. Okay, let's go. But the man took his time returning to his seat and stood there in the indefinite landscape of dark sky and black spruce.

The man then told a story of a couple of small-time thieves, without ambition, two jewel thieves who had a gun, just in case. Two friends of his who dreamed about crossing the border one day and heading south. A short time before the outage, a robbery had turned sour and the two partners in crime were running downtown in broad daylight, chased by a security guard. It was noon, and the streets were full. They slipped into the crowd, but behind them the strident sound of the whistle came closer and closer. Then the door to a laundromat opened and closed three times. A few moments later, the slower of the two robbers, the older one, had his cheek against the cold ceramic floor while a breathless man insulted him and put him in cuffs. Meanwhile, the younger of the two colleagues observed the scene through the porthole of a washing machine's drum, holding on to the revolver for dear life. Then the power went out. And a few days later, when the man returned home, after walking two hours in dreary streets that already smelled of chaos, she had left. Without warning.

It was dark. I worked to stay attentive. I drank my beer in small mouthfuls and watched the white line climb towards me, tossing its hips under the glare of my headlights. Despite the man's stories, I felt the boredom of a numb body trying to stay steady while my mind simply absented itself for long periods of time, without anyone noticing.

A sign of life. Or almost. Three loaded lumber trucks were parked on the side of the road. Clearly abandoned. I slowed down. The scent of cut wood made me think that if I were to commit a theft I wouldn't bother hitchhiking on trains, I'd steal one of these truckloads of wood and drive straight into the forest with it, as far as possible, and build myself a house next to a small lake or river. And I'd survive in peace, living off hunting and fishing and berries I picked.in summer.

The man asked us what we would do if the power never came back. The woman answered it was the least of her worries. Her answer seemed forced. I added that I'd cross that bridge when I got to it. The man laughed, there won't be a getting-there, the future is behind us, where are you going to hide, if the civil war breaks out?

KILOMETRE 3921

We passed a few houses. Squat homes covered in ugly vinyl siding. It was almost night and I kept my eyes open for cars without headlights. In the rear-view mirror I only saw the red ember of a cigarette, moving. Our impromptu passenger was telling the story of an old man who lived on the fourteenth floor. When the new year started, the man hadn't sent his rent cheques to cover that year's lease. He was sent a notice. Then warnings. And threats of eviction. One day, the concierge of the tower knocked at his door. Knock knock knock. No answer. The next week, he got the door broken in. Not a noise in the apartment. Not a hint of life. Only a dried-up silhouette, mummified in the immaculate solitude of bedsheets.

Suddenly, after a short silence, the man announced that we were almost there. I told him to speak up when he wanted me to stop. He put his hand on my shoulder, telling me that it was only a slight detour. I told him I still had a lot of road ahead of me and it was best to take advantage of the night to drive in peace. But he insisted. Speaking to the woman, he said that a little break couldn't hurt. That he knew a well-organized place, without danger. That he had friends there. We needed to rest at some point and driving any longer would just be dangerous.

I wasn't so sure. For now, I simply accelerated with the impression that my car was a raft adrift. That I steered the wheel of oblivion.

He added that his friends had a clandestine bar not too far away. A small bar where you could have a bit of fun, even during catastrophes. Then seeing that I didn't react, he raised his voice a little and offered to take the wheel. I glared at him for a moment in the rear-view mirror and, when I turned my eyes back to the road, I saw only the imprints of all the insects dead in mid-flight, shooting stars that ended their course on my windshield.

The man asked me whether I was awake enough to react if, all of a sudden, the woman stretched her arm out and pulled on the wheel, the car careening into a deep river after smashing through a guardrail. Without waiting for my answer, he said that was how he'd met the love of his life. Returning from a party. Alcohol, speed, music. Heavy eyes. The wheel slipping through his fingers. Steel screaming. The car flipping over. The fall. The surface of water like concrete. The slow sinking towards the deep. Impossible to open the doors because of the pressure. Silence. Panic. Air running out. Water rising. Obscurity. Elbowing the window. Water flooding into the car like a torrent. The last air pocket. The interminable and painful swim to the dancing lights of the surface. Then the intoxication of survival, in each other's arms.

Weighing his words, the man offered to buy us a few drinks and find us a room where we might sleep. He also told me he could find gas. I turned my eyes towards the woman, who finished her beer. She gestured that we should continue. I shrugged.

We were nearing an intersection. The man told me to turn right. I told myself again that if I hadn't been so damn thirsty, I would have kept on driving. He told me to slow down, that it was right there. I waited, kept on driving, and pulled on the steering wheel at the last possible moment. The car skidded on the road and the man tumbled against the seat back. He straightened himself, not saying a word, and lit a cigarette. The woman chuckled. The smile on her lips gave me some satisfaction even though I'd scared myself. For an instant I saw myself smashing into a tree, the airbag deploying, and my beer exploding in my face.

We were driving down a secondary road. Like everywhere else, there were no lights around us, except for the discreet glow of oil lamps in a few houses.

The man told us he had story for us, the last one.

Four in the morning, in the middle of summer. Two men went off to fish. The lake was covered in a quiet, oily fog. The sun was about to pull itself over the mountains. The catch had been particularly good in the few weeks prior. One man mechanically pulled on the oars while the other prepared his line. As their boat split the lake's soft surface, something seemed to follow in their wake. The oarsman saw this shimmering from the corner of his eye, stopped moving, and concentrated on the water's surface. An undulating and sinuous shape was headed for them. Alerted by his comrade's shout, the other fisherman turned around and discerned the same strange thing. They barely had time to realize what it was when the silhouette disappeared underwater, only a few metres from their boat. Panicked, both men scanned the water. Nothing. Only the short lapping of wavelets against their boat broke the silence. Convinced they'd be flipped into the water from one moment to the next, both men watched for the immense shadow that was surely turning beneath them, preparing its attack. Each man picked up an oar and they sat back to back, as if to protect each other. As they adjusted their positions, however, one man lost his footing and, as he tried to regain his balance, their boat capsized. The two men immediately began swimming towards the shore, convinced that this was it for them. But they made it ashore and survived. And in the following days they told the town's inhabitants about the lake monster, photographed a long time ago. He truly exists, they said. When the local media came asking questions, they had a perfectly forged story to tell. The monster hunted them. They were forced to abandon ship to avoid being swallowed whole by the beast. It was a miracle the beast let them live. A miracle and an honour! They appeared on the local news for a while, then were forgotten. But years later, on his deathbed, the man who'd taken the picture that had convinced so many across the globe that they were seeing indisputable proof of some prehistoric mystery admitted to his loved ones they shouldn't be too gullible because, on this earth, a small lie can turn other honest men into liars.

I told him to shut up. And when I raised my eyes to the rear-view mirror, I saw his eyes glow with the lucidity of inebriation. He told me to keep driving.

We entered a deserted village. While the man gave me directions, I heard the fingers of the woman tapping against the window, the coughing of the engine, and the clinking of empty beer bottles. We crossed a bridge and followed a river and only the foam of the water's eddies seemed to illuminate our surroundings.

We arrived at a two-storey building tucked away in the forest. The light of a bare bulb over the entrance illuminated the place. We exited the car one after the other. I unfolded myself with difficulty, thinking of the jaws of life. There were several vehicles in the parking lot, and the ground was marked with deep ruts. A few silhouettes moved here and there in the deeper dark, in the shadow of the moonless, starless night. In the distance, I heard the rumbling of the river. The man offered me a cigarette, and told me I was being foolish. That it was the sound of the generator. He turned and tried to caress the woman's cheek, but she backed up a few steps. He grabbed his hockey bag, his guitar case, and his beers, knocked on the hood of the car, crossed the small group amassed at the entrance, and disappeared inside.

When the door to the bar swung open, we heard music. The woman asked whether I really wanted to go inside. I told her the man had promised he'd find gasoline for us. Perhaps we'd learn more about what was going on. We wouldn't stay long at all, there was still too much road left before us. She looked at the ground for a moment and then, as if she'd suddenly dug deep and found a reserve of strength, pulled me by the hand towards the strange establishment.

I leaned against the bar in front of a mirror that doubled images of the bottles of hard alcohol, my beer, and my face. The woman was standing by my side. The place was noisy. Voices losing their way, glasses clinking, people looking at each other, bodies moving against one another. Through the thick fog of cigarette smoke floating at eye level, everything seemed normal. As if the past few days had all been a dream.

At the far end of the smoke-filled room, a few formerly purple couches where a few bodies had settled. The walls were covered with old posters surrounded by neon lights and dusty hunting trophies. We numbered about forty or so, nonchalantly gauging one another, halfway between a beer and a cigarette.

But our road companion wasn't among us.

I sensed that the woman wanted me to talk to her. Tell her some fun story. I couldn't tell a story for the life of me, and I wasn't in the right mood, anyway. I thought about my father, prisoner to his failing memory. His panicked voice over the phone. The power outage that seemed so far from where we were.

I stared at the ashtray as if something would emerge from it. But nothing. Seeing my empty beer, the barman stopped his back-and-forth in front of me.

Same thing? Sure, same thing, twice.

A bit farther up the counter, a mustachioed man curved over his glass as if he wanted to protect it. His lips moved without sound. His hollow cheeks and tight face were sculpted with precision. I observed him, thinking that I might end up like him. The barman returned and gave me two beers.

Here. You know where I might make a phone call? A phone call! Forget about it, you'll have more luck with smoke signals.

The mustachioed man turned towards us saying that landlines were out in most cases, but that cellphones still worked. I looked at the barman.

That's true? Yeah, it's true. Do you have one? Maybe, do you have money? Maybe. Follow me.

I told the woman to wait for me for a moment. I wouldn't be long. The barman led me into a small room at the back. And closed the door behind me.

Three men were seated at a low table. One of them asked me what they could do to help.

I'd like to make a phone call. It's important? Yes, it's important. You have what's needed? How much do you want?

They glanced at each other.

Two hundred dollars. Two hundred dollars! Take it or leave it.

I staggered back to the bar as if I'd just taken a punch to the face. The woman asked me what was wrong. I swallowed a mouthful of beer and told her I'd just wasted my time and money. That you couldn't trust anyone anymore. And that I was far too naive. She said I shouldn't worry and suggested that we return to the road soon, without paying, before the man came back. His promises were worth nothing. Then I felt her soft black eyes over my body. And her hand on the back of my neck.

And then her fingers walking across my back, delicately tracing the contours of my vertebrae.

I told her I'd like to be somewhere else. That I'd love to flee, far away. With her. Far from this bar. Far from this interminable road. Far from the damn car. I told her all we needed to do was to steal a truckload of wood, then go build ourselves a cabin in the woods, far away. On the shore of a lake. She turned her head slightly, smiled, and whispered that it was a good idea.

A few tables away from us, two young men spoke, gesticulating. The woman listened attentively to the words coming out of their mouths. She asked whether I understood what they were saying. I answered that people were in their words what they weren't in their silences. She laughed. She laughed and fatigue, which had been chasing us through the empty bottles, flamed for a moment before receding again.

I finished my beer. My heart was pumping clear blood. I felt lighter. I signalled to the barman. He took the two empty bottles, telling me I drank for two. I answered he hadn't seen anything yet.

The woman asked for a cigarette. I was looking for my cigarettes when we saw our passenger making his way towards us, holding his pack. His cheeks were red, his smile yellow, and his eyes gleaming. He asked for a beer and lit a cigarette. The woman got up and told me it was time to go. The man suggested she shouldn't go too far, that they had to settle first. He then glanced at me and put his arm around my shoulders. He thanked me and asked the bartender to bring me another beer. He warned me they wouldn't be long. And that it would be best for me if I stayed out of it. Getting up, he slipped a fifty-dollar bill into my shirt pocket and wished me luck. The woman made me understand I shouldn't make anything of it. Then the man led her towards the far end of the bar.

I stayed alone at the bar, watching them from the corner of my eye. But the music was too loud and there were too many people for me to understand what they were saying. Or understand what was happening. I drank, and beer evaporated from my bottle as people around me laughed and talked. Behind me, the two young men were still talking. Talking. Smoking. They were getting louder. Words one on top of the other. Louder and more aggressive. Then they stopped talking. And they drank.

I could feel the barman watching me, as if suspicious. But as long as he picked up my empty bottles and brought me back full ones, I didn't care.

The woman and the man were still in the corner of the room. I couldn't look away from them, except to take a swig of beer. Abruptly, the man pushed the woman towards the door. They went outside. I quickly got up and made my way after them. Walking down the stairs, I heard them bellowing at each other like two vultures fighting over roadkill. The man pointed his finger at me and shouted that this didn't concern me at all. The woman nodded and told me she'd prefer it if I went back in.

I turned around and made my way back to the bar. I drank. And as always, it helped. But it didn't turn anything off.

On the wall, a large moose head looked back at me with its glassy eyes. Around me, the whole roomful of people seemed stuffed. It had nothing to do with the power outage, I knew; it was just the way people moved at this time of night. I easily recognized the fatigue that clung to their eyes, dragging down the lines of their faces into the hollowness of their cheeks, on the corner of their lips. The same features I saw in the mirror.

The woman hadn't come back yet. I asked the barman whether he knew the man. He answered that he had no idea who I was talking about. I emptied my beer. Enough. It was time to go.

I got up too quickly and stumbled, my foot catching on the stool. I leaned against the table of the two young men behind me and, as I tried to regain my balance, the table folded under me and I crashed with it to the ground.

I opened my eyes. The barman's face was perched over mine. I told him that everything was fine and got to my knees as well as I could among the pieces of broken glass, spilt beer, and cigarette butts. He took me by the arm. I told him to leave me alone. I heard the two young men making fun of me. My head hurt. There was blood on the ground. The barman pulled me to my feet. I pushed him back and I told everyone to fuck off. Then I fought to find my composure, stood straighter, and walked to the bathroom, leaning against the wall.

Red streaks on the sink's white enamel. I lifted my head and looked myself straight in the eyes. My beard was already long, my eyes deeply bagged, and blood ran from my scalp to my chin.

What am I doing here?

By now I should have been with my father. In the mirror, I could barely recognize his face in my own. Did he have, at my age, that balding forehead, too-thick eyebrows, and hair the colour of ash? A face made of bags under the eyes and prominent veins, supported by a neck that knew how to discreetly swallow saliva? That washed-out air, held together by a jaw muscled from holding in so many yawns? Probably. But I couldn't remember. That was why I wanted to see him. Now. I didn't want to be just a name on the other side of the world. He needed me, I knew that. Even if he had always been stubborn, he would never be able to make it on his own, now. Especially with the outage. His memory was no longer anything but chalk on a blackboard. And I needed him as well. To make sure I looked as little like him as possible.

Someone was heading for the urinals. I steeled myself and turned on the tap, but no water came out. I soaked up the blood on my face as best I could with a paper towel. It was going to be okay.

I pushed the bathroom door open and the buzzing of music filled me again. The barman counted his bills and watched me from the corner of his eye. I slowly made my way to the exit. Passing by the bar, I noticed that the man was seated at my old stool. I walked up to him and asked him where the woman was. The barman stopped counting his bills. The man told me he didn't know. He was taunting me. I advised him to make an effort before I helped him remember. He jumped off the stool, warning me that I looked like I had drunk too much. I said he had no idea what he was talking about. And that he was terrible at telling stories. He took a drag of his cigarette and told me softly that was nothing, that I had never met his father. He said that I was still bloody, right there, under the temple.

Where is she?

The barman asked me whether I was talking to him. I shook my head and stared straight at my passenger.

Where is she?

The man said that she'd probably left without me. That sometimes life was sad, but that's just how it was. I stepped towards him. He dropped his cigarette butt to the ground. I tightened my fist. I threw myself at him. He dropped. My knuckles split open against the bar. I shouted. People turned and stared. I got back up and tried to hit him again. But he dodged one more time. Then the two young men jumped me, threw me to the ground, hit me, shouted that I was crazy. The barman came up and asked me what my problem was. As they dragged me to the back door, I raised my head and took a last look at the bar. The woman wasn't there, and the man had disappeared.

I was thrown out onto pavement. Through the insults, I could hear a voice ordering me never to come back here and another telling me that I should count myself lucky. That they'd gotten real mad for lesser offences. Then nothing at all, except the sound of a metal lock turning and the steady rumbling of the generator.

A clammy wetness shook me from my inertia. I shivered. My ears were ringing. Used to noise as I might be, used to the strident bark of tools, to tinnitus, last night's music played in a continuous loop in my skull like a broken record. It was morning. Very early. I had slept. I slept curled up there, among the garbage bags and wet cardboard.

I struggled to my feet and slowly made my way around the deserted building. It was still before sunrise. Behind me, the couch grass grew to the edge of a forest strewn with automobile carcasses. I listened closely. The generator was no longer working but I could still hear shouting from inside the bar. I'd better leave.

The woman.

She must have run away. I walked to my car. Unless she was hiding somewhere. The thickness in my mouth gave me nausea, but it would pass, everything would be okay. Or perhaps she'd left with the man after all?

No.

I stopped near my car, inspecting it quickly. Nobody had slashed the tires, broken a window, or stolen the luggage tied to the roof. No one had put sugar in my gas tank either. I hoped.

Leaning towards the door, I saw her, she was there. Hugging her knees and sleeping on the car seat, in one of my work vests. I opened the door. She woke up, startled, and asked where I'd been. I raised an eyebrow and told her I needed a coffee. She moved over to the passenger seat, staring at me the whole time. As soon as I sat down, I saw the state of my face in the rear-view mirror. She asked what had happened. I pushed away the hand she stretched towards me and told her it was nothing, that I'd seen worse. I turned the key and the engine started without hesitation.

We got back on the road. The sky was covered. The clouds low. And we passed no one. Perfect conditions. I thought about last night. The detour had cost me a lot. There were still too many kilometres to go. I would need to make sure I still had enough money left. But that could wait.

My head wanted to burst.

It was a drab day, a diffuse light soaked the grey asphalt. A day without sun other than a hazy disk that roved the sky behind clouds. On the shoulder, in ditches, garbage coloured the scenery. I accelerated. It was hard to bend my elbow and change speeds. When we reached the main road, the woman was once again immersed in deep sleep. Let her sleep. It was still early. She was so beautiful. And I had nothing to say. In fact, seeing her sleep there, next to me, made me feel just a bit more rested.

Her long black hair covered the seat's old fabric. A stage curtain after a turbulent play. I almost felt like applauding. Despite my bruises, I felt strangely good. I swallowed my headache. She was by my side.

She was by my side.

The sky was covered with a felt mass through which nothing could be distinguished from anything else, except, perhaps, the tips of pine trees that covered the hills.

I held the course steadfastly, but I couldn't tell whether the slow drum roll of the cracked asphalt would keep me awake or hypnotize me. I told myself once again that I cared not at all for the lascivious call of bedsheets. Conifers flew by on both sides of the car. The forest was dense. And we only went deeper.

The woman stirred, woke up, and turned towards me, smiling timidly. I thought about the dried blood on the side of my face, my open knuckles. She told me we should stop at the next town, that we should find what I needed for my injuries. That I looked like a madman who read too many stories of heroes on impossible quests.

We were getting closer to the city. Between settlements now, there were fewer and fewer kilometres of forest. If everything went well, in the next few hours, we would see the silhouettes of skyscrapers appear on the horizon. We were currently in one of the many towns of the area, in front of a strip mall along Main Street. There was a lot of activity around us. People coming and going in stores with broken front windows. Others filled their cars with boxes of supplies carried from their houses. Farther away, a man was recycling wood off a former billboard. Everything seemed to be happening at once, with a strange mixture of calm and chaos. No one paid us any attention. The woman got out of the car and made her way towards the pharmacy. The door had been forced open. She looked around, then went in.

She returned with peroxide, ointment, and a box of bandages. She told me to turn my head, and not move. That it might sting a little. I let myself be worked on while she told me how the pharmacy hadn't really been looted. That whoever had forced the door had only taken the basics. Cleaning the wounds on my knuckles she asked me what had happened. I quickly answered that some man, someone I didn't know, had taken a dislike to me for no reason. And that it had ended poorly. She stifled a laugh. I added that if she hadn't been in the car this morning, I would have left without her. And she was the one who owed me an explanation.

Tying the bandage around my hand, she said she owed me nothing. That we were going in the same direction, in the same car, and that was it.

I didn't say anything after that.

When I lifted the keys to start the car, she stopped my hand and leaned in to press her body against mine. I went to push her away, but she begged me to stop pretending. And I let her hands move over my torso until her lips were pressed against mine. Her warm lips. I pulled her to me, lifting her by her hips. And, a moment later, the interior or the car became very humid, and very cramped. Time no longer existed.

The car carried us across the tough and thorny hills. I took the long curves slowly, my head slightly angled and eyes deeply set on the lustrous asphalt.

Far away, orange signs rose between the grey sky and black asphalt. Construction. We drove slowly past the strange machines abandoned on the road. Dump trucks, pavers, and steamrollers all looked like bronze dinosaurs at the entrance to a museum. The woman sketched a smile and said we might as well change vehicles. I answered that nothing beat my car. But secretly, I was relieved to see the road was still accessible, despite the half-finished roadwork.

The forest surrounded us in a calculated way. As if it was slowly trying to take back from the road what clear cuts had taken away from it, farther north. I told the woman that this road would lead us directly to the city. She told me she knew. Then after a moment's silence, she admitted that she'd known the man we'd picked up the previous day. I turned towards her, but could only see her silhouette backlit by the grey light. She would have preferred never to see him again, she said. That no matter what she did, fate had always held a grudge against her.

The wind blew harder now. I could see it shaking the small trees on the side of the road and felt it beating against the sides of my car. The woman continued her story. She told me he was a ghost from her past life, a friend of her ex-boyfriend who'd become her lover. After the accident. That she'd pretended to not recognize him, at first, but it was already too late. She knew that someone would be sent to look for her. That there might be a reward. And that was the reason why he didn't want to let her go.

I listened to the woman, with my hands so tight on the wheel that I wouldn't have been able to react if something suddenly had jumped in front of us from out of the woods. She insisted that there was no danger now, that he wouldn't be following us. That everything had been settled. I looked up to the rear-view mirror. The road was long behind us, and empty.

I asked her whether it was because we were nearing the city that she admitted these things to me now. No. Good, because we can't know for sure what state the city will be in, I replied. She answered that, one way or another, the city would be her finishing line. But with everything she'd heard, she didn't know what to expect now. She then said that the approaching city wasn't the reason for her confession. Instead, it was because had she bought the man's silence by giving him the money from the bag under my seat.

I stopped the vehicle on the shoulder at the side of the road. There was nothing around us. A deserted road and wooded land.

I told the woman to get out.

She told me that it wouldn't make a difference now anyway. A few hundred dollars wouldn't have made a difference.

I reminded her that it was all I had left. That I was still a day of driving away from my father. I would need gas. Everything had become far too expensive now.

Speaking through the open window, the woman told me that she hadn't had a choice. That she could get out of the car here, if that's really what I wanted, but that she thought, in any case, that our fates were sealed. With or without money.

We reached the periphery of the city. It was littered with cars. The majority of them had been abandoned on the side of the road. We also saw, here and there, small groups of people. Some searched through abandoned cars while others walked on heavy feet, staring as we drove past.

The highway ran straight downtown. But for now, we followed the drab decor, seen so many times in the outskirts of all major cities. Parking lots like oil spills around warehouses. Vacant lots made of fences, gravel, and brambles. Entire neighbourhoods of cookie-cutter houses planted just off the highway. And immobile cranes, stretching their necks over construction sites.

As we approached, we noticed three helicopters circling downtown. We watched the flight of the metal beasts in a sky the colour of lead. Like birds of ill omen. Perhaps we should change our itinerary. But I wasn't yet sure what to do. Meanwhile, I had to drive even more carefully to avoid the debris strewn here and there on the road.

The woman pointed out, in the distance, several smouldering buildings, of which were left only burned-out skeletons. I had the impression that the city was pregnant with the stagnant chaos that comes after a huge storm. That we had arrived after some great rout. And we'd need to find a way to deal with whatever we would encounter.

I flew from one lane to another, making my way among abandoned cars and ripped-up luggage left on the highway. But despite my best weaving and bobbing, soon enough, we were forced to stop. A long line of immobile vehicles blocked the way. It was impossible to go any farther.

We got out of the car. Beyond the whap of the helicopters, several kilometres away, the city basked in a strange silence, punctuated by muted sounds and metallic yawning. Without a word to each other, we began walking towards the overpass that stretched out before us. In order to find a path though the inert traffic jam we had to, more than once, close car doors that had been left ajar. From the top of the viaduct, the line of vehicles seemed interminable. Like an arrow shot into the heart of this city abandoned to its own ghosts. We heard the echo of three gunshots. It seemed more like the last rumble of thunder in a departing storm. Except for a few wandering silhouettes in the unrecognizable streets, it seemed like all human activity had been suspended. Garbage bags strewn everywhere. The first floor of most buildings had been barricaded. Factory smokestacks silent, impotently pointing to the skies. And we couldn't hear a single emergency siren. I didn't dare imagine what the richer neighbourhoods might look like.

The woman moved forward a dozen steps, scanning the desolation. When she turned towards me, I asked her whether our journey together ended here. As she was preparing to answer, I noticed someone watching us from below. As I pointed my finger at him, he bellowed something inaudible and immediately disappeared. The woman indicated we'd talk later. And that for now it might be more prudent to return to the car.

I walked, scanning my surroundings. On the ground, I found a piece of flexible hose and said that it was as good a time as any to fill up on gas. When we reached our car, I told the woman to add oil to the engine. That she'd find a pint of it in the back. Meanwhile, I grabbed the jerry can and made my way to an abandoned truck. I unscrewed the cap, stuck the hose in, and sucked deeply until I had a vile taste in my mouth. I had to siphon four cars to fill the jerry can.

Walking back to my own car, I noticed that my companion wasn't there. I didn't dare call out to her for fear of attracting unwanted attention. She might have left anyway. Just like that, without saying thanks. Like a thief in the night. Egotistic. Traitorous.

Without wasting time, I brought up the gas canister to the gas tank. And once again I noticed the woman waiting for me, sitting in the car's passenger seat. When she noticed me, she became agitated as if I had surprised her. At the same moment I heard footsteps behind me. I turned around. A man about my size was walking towards me, holding an iron bar.

What do you want? Don't yell, you could attract the others, and then I would have to shut you up. What do you want? Your gas, your water, and your food, quickly, give it all. I don't have water or food. You're lying, come on. Hurry.

The man walked towards me, threatening. When he came close enough, I splashed the contents of the jerry can at him. Then, before he had time to jump me, I took out my lighter and told him that if he walked one step closer, he'd burn.

The man hesitated a moment, gave his clothes a sniff, and began backtracking slowly, cursing me out. He climbed onto a bike he'd left on the ground a bit farther off and disappeared. I quickly poured the rest of the gas into the tank, jumped into the car, and started it up. We began to back up, mindful of trash and hunks of metal. We passed a few groups of people on our way out. Without thinking about what they were doing, what they might be looking for, or who they might be waiting for along the highway, we drove onto a ring road that led eastward, through the suburbs.

My hands were clammy and my heart was in my throat. I felt weak. I thought I might vomit.

KILOMETRE 4232

There was a lot more action near the city. A whole lot more cars driving. No one respected any of the road signs, but everyone drove slowly. We followed the pack, watching the houses go by. Some had been burned and were still smoking. Others were walled in by makeshift palisades made of road signs, wire fences, and wooden planks. But most seemed simply abandoned.

My shirt smelled like gasoline. I asked the woman to hold on to the wheel while I took off my shirt. She told me that everything would have gone up in flames if I'd actually tried to light my attacker on fire. I threw the shirt out the window, grabbed another from the backseat, and took control of the wheel. I turned towards the woman. I nodded.

We crossed a bridge. A sign had been placed between the concrete blocks. PREPARE TO STOP. We passed in front of a sentry box placed in the middle of the road. Probably a makeshift checkpoint. It had been deserted. The cones and barricades had been tossed to the ground. I accelerated. I was driving with the uneasy certainty of being followed even though, in the rear-view mirror, all I saw were anonymous vehicles, rundown billboards, and skyscrapers, slowly pulling away. We took an off-ramp that led to a road that followed the river for hundreds of kilometres before forcing its way into the eastern forest. The road that would lead me to my father. By tomorrow.

On the other side of the river, I recognized the city port, but I'd never seen so many containers waiting on ships and in triage yards. From this side of the river, we could see people seated on the concrete guardrail, fishing, watching the movement of helicopters. I was startled by the woman's hand on my thigh. She leaned towards me and told me that she'd accompany me to my destination. That I no longer had a choice. That she would help me find my father. I smiled and told her she was the one who no longer had a choice.

Then she kissed me.

Little by little, we left behind us the city's people and infra-structure and drove in silence, midway through apprehension of what lay ahead of us and relief at not being alone. And even perhaps at being together.

On the horizon, clouds gathered and seemed to want to hem the landscape in, as if a giant hand was about to take hold of the world. Soon, between earth and sky, there would be room only for the space of a car.

Night already. The road followed its path through farmland and, from the flood plain through which we were driving, we could see the black line of the river growing thicker, in the distance. I counted the time, my speed, and the distance left to go. Then I measured my fatigue, feeling the pain in the muscles of my neck.

I said we should take a break. We could try to find some gas, eat some food. Rest. The woman answered it might be best to wait a bit before stopping. That what we'd seen today made her fear traps, ambushes. I took her hand. It was cold.

She offered to drive. She said that I had a funny look about me with my black eye and my bandaged hand. I was probably exhausted.

I answered that I was okay. For now. But my mouth was dry and my words were barely audible. Each time I coughed, the car pulled sideways. Along curves, I knew the guardrails kept a close eye on me.

Under the grey cloth of twilight, I could barely make out the outline of old mountains. I realized it must have rained today. Potholes were filled with water.

A fine fog began to settle. The woman asked me what would happen when we got there. I would have liked to give an answer, but I simply had no idea.

I drove, staring directly into night's gaze. I could feel fatigue like an itch under my tongue. I turned on the headlights. But they too were exhausted, lighting not much more than an arm's length in a dark corridor.

I concentrated on my driving, but beyond the layers of fog released from the peaks of trees, only the glowing eyes of wild animals showed the way.

KILOMETRE 4535

The road was no more than a thin line between the mountains on one side and the river widening into an inland sea on the other. We couldn't see any of it, of course, with night around us, but the salt air didn't lie. The car split the fog and I had the impression, every so often, of hearing waves crash on the front bumper. Night was deep. Opaque. We crossed it slowly, one kilometre at a time, the dashboard lights sparkling.

My vision began to cloud. For a second, I felt as though I wasn't there. To see properly, I had to wipe the windshield with my sleeve over and over again. Between towns, where houses nestled in the hollows of coves, I could imagine the dancing light of candles. The road followed the coastline closely. Pushed by the wind, the sea crashed onto the road. One after the other, waves surprised by the headlights froze for an instant in the air before letting themselves collapse on the asphalt. They looked like sea monsters trying to reach out of the deep to demolish us.

As we advanced on the soaked road, I sensed the inside of the car narrowing. Despite my grip on the wheel, the muscles of my neck always ended up relaxing, as if I was deserting my post. Each time I straightened my head, I had the impression that these microseconds lasted an eternity.

Morning now. A strange dawn pierced the fog. I parked next to my father's car, which was so old and big you might easily confuse it for a boat. I turned off the engine and ripped out of my seat. A few paces took me across the rotten steps of the front stoop. The woman stayed in the car. The door was half-open. It's me! No answer. I walked from one room to the next. The kitchen was filled with empty tin cans. And the furniture in the living room had been tipped over. Hello? No answer. I climbed to the second floor. The staircase was dusty and dirty. It seemed like nobody had been here in weeks. From the hallway, I saw that my father's bed was unmade and empty. I wanted to go into my old room, but the door was locked. Where are you? Tell me, where are you?

The woman shrieked. I opened my eyes and pulled on the steering wheel. The tires drew ruts in the gravel, the car zig-zagged and found the road, barely. My heart pulsed all the way to the tips of my fingers. A moment longer and we would have crashed into the ditch.

I turned my head towards the woman. I'm sorry. She offered me a cigarette, telling me to smoke. That it would keep me awake. Trying to hide the tremors that shook my hands, I tried to convince myself that my reflexes had saved our lives.

I was thirsty. I thought about the beers I drank the previous night. They helped me feel better, despite everything that had happened. I was ready for another round. I concentrated on the road. Night spread out before us. My pupils dilated to the point of bursting out of my eyes but the fog remained, impassable. It seemed like my headlights were dimming, little by little. I looked straight ahead, clicking my tongue against the roof of my mouth. I was thirsty.

We passed under the dark streetlights of a small riverside town. I tried to hold myself together, but my body was heavy. Numb. Subterranean. The weight of kilometres crushing me. I thought of my father, prisoner of his amnesia, of old age, and of the darkness of his village. I feared that the panic caused by the power outage stopped him from knowing what was real and what wasn't. That he had fled somewhere. Or barricaded himself in his house. I feared he might be suspicious of me, that he might not recognize me. We hadn't seen each other in more than ten years. And I couldn't tell anymore whether I was dragging my past behind or being chased by it.

The woman offered to take the wheel once again. I repeated that everything was fine, that I was steady, that we were almost there. And then a light winked on my dashboard.

We needed to find gas. Fast.

I stopped at the first house we saw. I told the woman we shouldn't make any noise. It was past midnight. There were two cars in the yard, but we couldn't know how many people were sleeping under the roof, if any.

Knowing I'd need to covertly siphon gas was enough to revive me. As I got ready to pump gas out of one of the vehicles, the woman brought me a jerry can. As she reached me, I sucked through the tube three times, hard, and the canister slowly began to fill. We kneeled in the gravel and spoke softly. The woman pointed out that there was a thin trickle of smoke coming from the chimney. The house occupants had probably prepared their supper on the wood stove.

I said we could go and knock on the door. Ask for help. We would have done just that if things were as they used to be. But the woman replied immediately that things were definitely not as they used to be. That if someone came to knock on my door in the middle of the night, I would probably welcome him with the barrel of a gun.

The jerry can was full now. Stillness around us. We could hear waves crash against the sea wall, on the other side of the road. Deeper in the interior, through the mountains, I could hear the echoes of coyotes patrolling the forest. The woman told me I was wrong, that it was simply the whistling of wind through tree branches. I answered that just because we couldn't hear them wail didn't mean they weren't there.

I got up and began dragging the canister towards my car. It was heavy. I asked the woman to help me. I'm tired, I told her. She said she knew. Then she asked me whether we would have enough gas to make it to my father's. I thought so.

Before leaving, we both sat on the hood of the car. The night was cool, but under us, the hood was warm. Not far away, the sea churned, enshrouded in thick fog.

I listened closely, thinking I heard a car coming in the other direction. A few moments later, two headlights pierced the humid canvas of the night, heading straight for us. Suddenly, the woman grabbed me and pulled me into the hedge, ordering me to not make a move. Crouching under the branches, I realized I was so tired I could barely think. A car passed in front of us without slowing down. Coming out from under our hiding place, the woman said that circumstances often favoured those who remained circumspect.

It had started to rain. My body burned with weariness, and I shivered uncontrollably. I had the impression that the rain evaporated as soon as it touched me. I tried to wake myself up by jumping up and down, but the weight of my legs and arms was a clear enough sign that I couldn't manage another night of driving. The woman told me we'd better go before the house's inhabitants noticed us. I told her we should give it another minute. A gust of wind caressed the treetops and raised spindrift from the waves. A light drizzle fell. When I finally decided to make my way to the car, the woman quickly opened the door for me. On the passenger side.

Long tears of rain drew furrows on the windshield. The back-
and-forth of the wipers reminded me that everything could
disappear in a moment. I slowly sank into the seat, losing sight
of the washed-out landscape. I was soaked. My hair lay limply
against my face and my clothes clung to my body.

As we travelled through the dark and seeping night, I let
myself be driven, feeling like a stranger in my own car. I leaned
towards the woman and told her to be careful. It was an old
car, and capricious, but I liked it. And even if I had noticed
that the woman seemed to know intimately the particularities
of the old gearbox, I still kept a close eye on her.

She told me that everything would be okay, and insisted
I relax. She suggested that I look under the seat. I slipped my
hands under it as if scared to get bitten, and my fingers touched
something. I pulled out a bottle of clear and flammable liquid.
She told me she'd stolen it from the bar while no one was

looking, the bar where we'd left the man behind. That it was a present for the last few kilometres. A small gift. And that alcohol would calm me. At least a little.

My lips met the bottle, and I felt the path of the alcohol as it made its way to my stomach and into my veins.

The rain fell harder now, a muted din on the roof. We drifted away from the coast, and soon enough would be committing ourselves to a long thin corridor made of wild beasts and forest. Drops of water exploded on the asphalt like glass marbles on a slate floor. So many twinkling bursts of light like a clear night sky. But I'd never known how to find my path through a field of stars. When I watched a clear sky, at night, I never saw constellations. Only countless, nameless, tiny sparkling dots.

My eyelids felt heavy but I couldn't close them. There was no point, now, anyway. I counted the kilometres of the journey like the cars of a train longer than the breadth of my knowing. As I lit a cigarette, the woman grabbed the bottle from my hands and took a long swallow. The car was aimed at its destination like an arrow, the wheels barely touching the road now, shooting water from either side. I could hear the metal vibrating. I was surprised that my old car, like an unkillable old mare, was holding its own, barely a whimper heard.

The woman suggested that I sleep. I said that I couldn't. That we were almost there. She told me to tell her a story. Or hum something. Anything. That it would go faster. But I had neither the desire nor the energy.

We were moving as fast as the car could handle. In a forest. In the middle of the night. The engine's roar cradled me. And my body curved in on itself to the rhythm of the shaking of the road.

I was sleeping, then I wasn't. I observed, for a time, the alcohol making waves in its glass prison. I slept, I hadn't.

I had to hold on. We were almost there. Fifteen minutes maybe. Not much more than that. Maybe thirty minutes. To close my eyes. No. Another mouthful. I could barely taste it. Like water.

I wasn't sleeping. I couldn't. My mother had her accident on this stretch of road. I drank more. This is where she died, I thought. I didn't know anymore.

I was running on fumes. Dead tired.

The horn shrieked like a child whose imagination is playing tricks on him.

I raised my head and loosened my eyelids.

In front of me, two golden eyes watched the car come closer.

I turned my head towards the woman.

She stepped on the brakes with all her strength.

The scream of wheels on asphalt like a dream, slaughtered.

We were projected forwards.

She pulled on the wheel.

Water on the road.

Sideways now.

Antlers. No, two hands raised skywards.

A muted impact.

A silhouette knocked over.

White hair, rain boots, and a checkered shirt.

Cracks in the windshield.

Blood.
The car barrelling.
The bottle exploding.
My tools thrown inside the car like a sheet of metal rain.
The ditch. Bushes.
Metal folding with a shriek, the crying of felled trees.
The steering wheel like a punch in the stomach.
Airbags, too late.
Glass bursting.
My clothes torn. My head. My legs.
Then the pain of stillness.
The crackling of fire under the rain.
The car whistling, upside down, on the tall grass.
And silence circling in like a scavenger.

IX. ARIADNE'S THREAD

The golden fingers of dawn stretch over the labyrinth while, in the depths of the maze, the dust is only now settling. The young mercenary roams the corridors and galleries murmuring to himself: I killed the beast, I killed the beast. He is exhausted, but doesn't understand why there is no blood on his weapon or his hands. The only red objects around him are pieces of the woollen thread, slit by the sharp bronze of his sword and dispersed by his frantic chase.

Each time he raises his head, he believes he's found his path, suddenly knows how to uncover the hidden exit. This reassures him even if, in truth, he's doing no more than wandering a labyrinth that is slowly closing in on him.

PART
THREE

Under my spine, I felt the curvature of the earth, pieces of plastic and shards of wood.

Around me, rain pattered in the forest. Like applause after an intoxicating performance.

I wanted to stand and clap my hands in turn, but the car had bowled over my legs and the rest of my body was driven into the ground among the roots and dirt.

Water flowed onto my face and into my half-open mouth. After each breath, I had to either spit it out or swallow it.

The immensity of night slowly faded away and all that was left was a drab sky, needlepointed by the spiny arms of trees.

I heard voices and sounds approaching. In the deep grey obscurity, I saw lightning that didn't exist. The beams of flashlights coming closer. I would have liked to make a sign, a sound, but I couldn't move, could barely breathe. They'd see my car's carcass sooner or later. Or mine.

Behind my closed eyes, I could still hear my car's reassuring rumbling. I wanted to see my father. I had less than an hour left to go. Probably thirty minutes at most. But I was still thirsty. I wouldn't mind a drink of that clear liquid that strengthened my voice.

I slowly came to my senses. I opened my eyes. I wasn't at the wheel of my car. I was in bed, in a small room lit by a flickering oil lamp. I wondered where I was. And when. Time expanded in me like a hemorrhage. I had to leave. Return to the road. Find my father.

I eventually succeeded in raising my head. My legs were dressed in thick blood-soaked cloth. When I tried to move my toes, my body shuddered. I was in pain. An unbearable tingling. I tried to move and realized that my wrists were handcuffed to the bedframe.

There was a window in the room. But it had been covered by old planks. I waited. I had no choice. I saw a bunch of coats, hanging on the walls. Stacked boxes in a corner. Luggage. A pile of shoes and rain boots. Plastic covering. Rope. A chainsaw. And boxes of tools.

My tools.

Suddenly, through the wheezing of my breath, I heard voices in nearby rooms. I tried to concentrate and pick out a few words. But a fit of coughing overtook me and battered the fragile walls of my chest.

The door squealed. A man walked towards the bed before bending over me. He had a beard and his clothes were speckled with mud. We looked at each other for a moment, without saying a word, then he quickly left. The room was like a desert road after the rain. My gaze settled on the floor, pooling and spreading out like a puddle of dirty water made cloudy from the unexpected passage of a car.

The light of the oil lamp faded. Everything became dark in the room and the mess on the floor only made the shadows denser. And yet, when I closed my eyes – white light where memories should be – a blank slate. I knew I'd been driving for days. And nothing else. I knew that I'd been driving for so long that I thought I'd been flying. I knew that fatigue had ravaged me like a wild beast. And nothing. Nothing, except for this room and daggers of pain in my legs.

Two men came into the room and leaned their hunting rifles against the wall. They came nearer, asking me how I felt.

Blinded by their flashlights, I had nothing to say. A shudder of fear was my answer. I tried to get back up to a sitting position in my bed, but the handcuffs didn't leave me much room to move. The elder of the two ordered the other to go and get food and water. Then he inspected my injuries, his jaw tight.

Where am I? Don't worry about that, you're safe. Why am I handcuffed? You were agitated, we didn't know what to do, you were making your injuries worse. Who are you? What happened? One of our patrols found you unconscious on the side of the road and brought you back here, three days ago. I wasn't on patrol, but they told me you'd been in an accident. There are no doctors here, I take care of the sick and injured. You lost a lot of blood, but you'll pull through. Your knees are in pretty rough shape though, we'll see whether you can walk again. First, your fractures need time to heal. It should be okay though, or we'll figure out some other solution.

The man kept talking, but I'd stopped listening. Looking at his lips moving, I tried to understand what had happened. The accident. The accident? What accident?

Then I cut him off, searching avidly for his eyes. My father. My father. A phone. I need to make a phone call. It's important. He has to know I'm almost there. That I'm nearby. I need to call him. He'll come and get me.

The man looked me over, suspicious. As if he was afraid I'd attack him. Outside, it was still raining. I could hear water beating on the roof and running along the walls. It made me think of the oil that dripped out of my car.

I need to speak to my father! Where were you coming from, fleeing the city like all the rest? No, I need to make a phone call. Come now, you need to rest, we'll speak later. I can't, I won't get there in time. Calm down, you're confused, you're lucky that my men didn't leave you to rot under your car. Wait! Shut up.

And he closed the door solidly behind him while I vainly pulled on my chains.

I woke to the sound of jingling metal. A man about my age was undoing my handcuffs. He brought me water, a piece of bread, and a can of tuna. He told me it was time to eat and he stayed there, against the far wall, watching me, a revolver tucked in his belt. As I stared at the drab meal, rubbing my wrists, he began asking questions.

You came from far away? Did you get into the city? What's happening there? Why are you here? There's nothing here. How did you get into that accident? Was that the old mechanic who forced you off the road? When we found you, you looked as dead as the other guy, but you were still breathing. I don't know why, but your face reminded me of someone. I convinced the others to bring you back to camp.

I tried to get my thoughts in order. My father. The power outage. The road. The woman. The woman!

Where's the woman who was with me?

The woman? What woman? There was no woman. There was no one on the passenger side when we pulled you out of your car. We would have noticed if there'd been anyone else. Not the first time we've seen bodies. We only found the body of the old town mechanic, a bit farther away. A stubborn old bastard. We let him go a few days ago because no one could reason with him anymore. God, he was more trouble than he was worth. He kept saying he was looking for his wife. But his wife died a long time ago. A car accident. Everyone in town knew he was alone, that he was losing his memory, inventing stories. He had a son, but he's been gone for years. Anyway, he died instantly, the old man. We buried him near the site of the accident. Or we'd have coyotes roaming around for weeks. He isn't the first one to have lost his mind these days. Even if the power comes back on, nothing will ever be the same. We hear it's chaos in the city. That gangs took advantage of the disorder, looted, and created panic. Here things are a bit better, but it isn't easy. Survival forces us to go against certain people's sensibilities. You're not eating. You need to keep your strength up. You know, the more I look at you, the more you make me think of someone. Your face, I feel like I've seen it somewhere. Go on, eat, it isn't as if we have endless supplies. We need to go scavenging for food, after all. I know, didn't we go to elementary school together maybe? No matter. Everything's changed so much. Everything that's happened since the power outage destroyed whatever life we had before. We barely have a past now. But you can't be afraid. Here we might not know our past so well, but we're surviving. It's what we've always done. Anyway, come now, what's your name? Tell me your name.

TRANSLATOR'S NOTE

In *Running on Fumes* we witness a timeless tale, a myth both ancient and contemporary. The original French version, *Le fil des kilomètres* by Christian Guay-Poliquin, retells the myth of Theseus and the Minotaur in the present tense, a particularly francophone approach to storytelling. For my translation, I chose the past tense to describe the travels of our narrator, emboldened by despair, as he journeys across an increasingly strange post-apocalyptic landscape. We see a country recognizable in its physical architecture but changed and traumatized by an unnamed catastrophe of epic – in its truest sense – proportions.

Storytelling in French is more flexible in its use of tense than in English. Epic narratives in English tend to ascribe more meaning to tense; stories, and myths in particular, are told in the past. They are timeless, occurring now as well as then, and part of their timeless quality is a function of the tense we choose. Our predecessors would tell the story of Theseus as he journeys through the labyrinth for love and glory in the past tense, all the while relating to contemporary audiences of shared values, beliefs, and political challenges. In *Running on Fumes*, the same holds true. The events we experience serve as a warning for our current challenges. It is in this sense that the myth of Theseus is both timeless and current. In other words, we use the past tense to describe events that might be taking place now. While some contemporary literature challenges the long-held notion of past tense as the only choice for the storyteller, tradition still holds strong in the realm of myth.

Road novels are our modern-day myths. They are the embodiment of Joseph Campbell's concept of the monomyth. A strong lineage runs from the *Odyssey*, narrated millennia ago, to Jack Kerouac's *On the Road*, written decades ago, or Cormac McCarthy's *The Road*, written more recently; they all tell of the hero's journey as he is called to face a series of trials and is resurrected before reaching apotheosis or atonement. *Running on Fumes* is no different in the sense that our unnamed hero moves through these classic stages, though in our tale the backdrop of hooves beating dusty ground is changed for the hammering of pistons in a rusted engine.

My choice to use the past tense instead of the present in the translation of this story was not an easy one. In the end, I gave precedence to the fact that the story retells a myth and thus should reflect English-language literary traditions. Ours is a story that can be placed in any setting of time and place and still speak to a shared experience.

I hope *Running on Fumes* rings as true to you as it did to me, that our hero's journey seems faithful to our own pathways through scarred landscapes both within and around us, and that you accompanied our damned hero to the end, as he strives to find his way through the labyrinth of our world gone mad.

—JACOB HOMEL

ACKNOWLEDGMENTS

Warmest thanks to all those who contributed to this project and helped me keep this novel on the road. From one version to the next, they helped me see the straight lines, the turns, the precipices. They were my guardrails.

So thank you to Catherine Brunet, Nicolas Rochette, Antoine Joie, André Thomas, Réjean Guay, Pierre-Olivier Colombat, Laurence Granbois-Bernard, and Micheline Genest.

And special thanks to the writer Brigitte Caron who gave me her patient support from the very first kilometre.

JACOB HOMEL, born and raised in Montreal, has translated or collaborated in the translation of a number of works, including Nelly Arcan's *Hysteric* and *Breakneck*, Frédéric Bastien's *The Battle of London* and Hadrien Laroche's *The Last Genet*. In 2012, he won the J.I. Segal Translation Prize for his translation of *A Pinch of Time* by Claude Tatilon. He currently lives in Montreal.

CHRISTIAN GUAY-POLIQUIN was born just north of the U.S. border in Saint-Armand, Quebec, in 1982. He believes the art of the narrative is grounded in the demands and details of daily life, situated in a world ripe with experience. He is currently developing a doctoral thesis on the hunting narrative and writing his second novel, *Le poids de la neige*, forthcoming from La Pleuplade in September 2016. *Le fil des kilomètres* (La Peuplade, 2013), his first novel, was published in both Quebec and France.